Notes from the Undergrad

Notes from the Undergrad

Rob Thomas

Simon & Schuster Books for Young Readers

Thanks to Jeff DeMouy, Jenny Ziegler,
Michael Conathan, Robert Young,
Bob and Diana Thomas, Christine Edwards,
Greg McCormack, Loyd Blankenship,
Peter Miller, Olivier Bourgoin, Elena Blanco,
Jennifer Stephenson, Kim Ruiz, and Reneé Vaillancourt.
Special thanks to my editor, David Gale,
and my agent, Jennifer Robinson.

SIMON & SCHUSTER BOOKS FOR YOUNG READERS
An imprint of Simon & Schuster Children's Publishing Division
1230 Avenue of the Americas
New York, New York 10020
Text copyright © 1997 by Rob Thomas
SIMON & SCHUSTER BOOKS FOR YOUNG READERS
is a trademark of Simon & Schuster.
Book design by Symon Chow
The text of this book is set in 13 point Cochin
Printed and bound in the United States of America
First Edition
10 9 8 7 6 5 4 3 2 1
Library of Congress Cataloging-in-Publication Data
Thomas, Rob.
Doing time: notes from the undergrad/ by Rob Thomas
     p.   cm.
Summary: Each of these ten short stories focuses on a high school
student's mandatory 200 hours of community service and the
student's response to the required project.
ISBN 0-698-80958-1
1. Children's stories, American. [1. Voluntarism-Fiction.
2. High schools-Fiction. 3. Schools-Fiction. 4. Short stories.] 1. Title.
PZ7.T36935Do 1997 [Fic]-dc21 97-524 CIP AC

A version of "Loss of Pet" was originally published in *Seventeen*.
A version of "Box Nine" originally appeared on the *Austin Chronicle* Web site.

For Russell Smith —
Without you, I'm nothing.

Table of Contents

Shacks From Mansions

The words " . . . required community service projects . . . " come out of Dr. Shiring's mouth, and the rest of Social Work 322—well-intentioned sons and daughters of the eggplant-colored Aerostar set—bob their heads like they've got springs for necks. They think it's swell; I can tell already. Why even do the study? Let's just write our reports now. Save some time.

Dr. Shiring's hippie teaching assistant starts handing out cases. Nearly three hundred of them. Divided up for our class that means about nine each. The professor reviews the assignment.

"While it's been a long-standing tradition in private schools to require these projects, public schools have just begun to follow suit," she says. "There have even been some legal challenges to mandating this sort of work, but those court cases have all failed."

The T.A. plunks folders down on the flip-up desk on my auditorium seat and continues down the row. I glance at the files, but try to keep listening to Dr. Shiring.

"The seniors at Lee High School here in town had to complete two hundred hours of community service in order to graduate. The manila folders you're being handed now contain the essays they had to write, the documentation of their hours, and an evaluation they completed regarding the program."

Flipping through the files, I see I got a candy striper, a canned food collector, a toy driver, a library "volunteer."

"What I want you to do," Dr. Shiring says; I get my pencil ready, "is to take your nine, or in some instances ten, cases and make follow-up calls to the students involved. Interview them. Try to get more out of them than you see in that folder. Deerfield ISD has commissioned us to evaluate the success of the program."

Costas Tobin, of the Highland Park Tobins, who I'm sure either stumbled on the phrase "noblesse oblige" in a Kennedy biography or experienced some sort of spiritual conversion after failing out of the SMU business school, raises his hand like this is junior high or something.

"Costas?" Dr. Shiring says.

"How do we define 'success?'" he asks.

With a dictionary, I say to myself.

" . . . For the purpose of this report, I mean."

Sorry. It's a decent enough question, but the boy shouldn't be in the social work program in the first place. Reality is gonna take a huge chunk out of his ass the first time he tries to tell an angry young brother to "chill." He'll be back at Central Texas University working on that teaching certificate, applying to private schools that italicize the word "exclusive" in their brochures.

This one time, Costas gave me a ride back up to Dallas for a weekend—we'd just completed a mock intervention project together, and he'd heard I was looking for a way up to my sister's wedding. When we got to Dallas, I told him to drop me off at a McDonald's right on I-35, and I'd have someone come get me, but he begged to take me to my doorstep right in the middle of South Oak Cliff—a neighborhood newspaper columnists started calling "Little Rwanda" on account of all the dark-skinned people capping each other. Ten miles from Costas's Highland Park home, but it might as well as have been Venus.

"Ain't been to the hood in a long-ass time," he said. *Yeah, like since you were born.*

Then the guy insists on stopping at Big J's Liquors to pick up "some smokes." Eight blocks from my house, and the guy has got to show me his *Pulp Fiction* credentials, like people are gonna be impressed with his cool quotient.

So Costas pulls into this liquor store, parks his Audi. I follow him inside, morbidly curious. I've already had to listen to three hours of Arrested Development and admit I missed the Farrakhan special on BET. ("It was fly.") I'm half expecting him to try to "walk" a forty-ounce of St. Ides. He doesn't, but during the cigarette purchasing exchange he somehow manages to let Big J know that Tyson was framed. Big J looks at me. I shrug.

I got home safely.

"Nice crib," he said as we stepped inside my house.

I realized at that moment that all the textbooks in the world can't teach you what a life you haven't lived is all about. How could people like Costas ever really understand "charity" or "service" if they've only been on the giving end of it? To them it's *auctions, functions, balls, write-offs.* Somehow it even manages to make them feel good. What do they call it? Chicken soup for the soul? That's classic.

But I've been on the other side.

I was eight years old, and I didn't really under-stand it at first—why suddenly I had this "Big Brother." The first time he came to the house, I hid in my room and wouldn't come out. I feared strangers. I was weak in a neighborhood that devoured its own. The man was out in the front room listening to my mother. I could hear her *"I just don't understand*s" and *"since his father died*s."

"What do he like?" the man asked.

"He likes to read," Momma said.

"Read?"

"Books," she confirmed. "This really is going to be a treat for Randall. He certainly needs to spend some time around a man. It's just women in the house except for him. Oh, and he has nightmares something terrible, and at his age he shouldn't still be wetting the—"

With whatever pride an eight-year-old bed wetter can manage, I threw open the door before she could finish.

"There he is!" Momma said, as if my sudden appearance was a surprise. It took me years to figure out what a smart lady my mother was.

"Hey there, little man," said the stranger. But he wasn't a stranger. Not exactly. I knew him from somewhere. It took me a couple puzzled seconds to figure out where. I owned his card. His football card. This was Preston "The Thief" Moncrief, starting cornerback for the Dallas Cowboys. Led the NFL with eleven interceptions the year before.

"You're The Thief!" I said, thrilled so severely I was in danger of losing bladder control right there in front of him.

"Randall!" Momma said sharply.

"No, no, that's okay," Preston said. "Nickname."

He looked me square in the eye.

"Wanna go have some fun?" he said.

That afternoon we must have spent thirty dollars at a Malibu Grand Prix playing video games, *Defender* mainly. Folks would come up while we were saving the galaxy and try to get Preston's autograph, but he'd tell them they'd have to wait until the game was over. He'd sign the napkin or whatever they handed him, have me sign it, too, then put our high score on it. Like they were asking for both our autographs because we were such good astro pilots.

We did a bunch of stuff like that over the next few weeks: miniature golf, bowling, Six Flags, even. Sometimes he'd come by and pick me up from school. When he'd show up, everyone would crowd around his Jaguar and try to touch him or get his attention. He'd be nice, but after a few minutes, he'd say, "Randall, ready to roll?" Everyone would go *awwww*, and wish they were me. It was a strange feeling, but I decided I could get used to it.

Then, one time while everyone was gathered around the car, Stephawn Coleman tossed Preston a football and took off toward the jungle gym on the far side of the field. Preston let him go deep, then threw a bullet. Stephawn reached out and plucked the ball out of the air like cotton, tucked it under, faked a stiff arm, Cabbage Patched his way across the end zone in a pretty good imitation of Preston, and spiked the ball. Preston whistled.

"Boy got hands," he said. "Randall, you go out for one."

"C'mon, Preston, we better roll."

Stephawn came loping in with the football.

"Give it up, young buck," Preston said, holding his hand up to Stephawn. Stephawn pitched him the ball.

Preston gave me a look.

"Show us what you got, little man."

"He can't catch," Stephawn said.

"Or run," added one of the smiling hangers-on.

All Preston said was, "Go."

I hesitated, but he gave me a reassuring nod and

a little smile, so I took off. Sort of. My legs churned at the ground, but I hardly moved. I fantasized briefly about running fast enough that I would outrace his throw. I looked back and discovered that I hadn't put twenty yards between the pack and me. Preston hadn't even cocked the ball yet. Looking back was a mistake. My feet got all tangled up. I tripped and rolled. Playground stickers tore at my palms. I heard the laughter, stood, and regarded Preston with an "oh, well" shrug. I thought that was that, but he waved me deep.

There was this look in his eye like now he wasn't playing around. I plodded off in the direction of the high-bars, my palms stinging, tears in my eyes. The ball, when I saw it, was a brown blur accelerating down at me like some sort of bird of prey. If I could've, I would've just run away from it, pretended I'd cut the wrong way, but it was coming straight at me, unavoidable. I put my hands up to fend it off. I had no delusions of catching it.

The skin of the ball slid across my fingers just before the nose of the ball smashed into my mouth, splitting my lip and filling my mouth with blood. The force knocked me over onto my back. I don't remember the fall, just the howls of laughter as I lay there unable to get up.

Later, in the safety of the Jag, Preston tried to make me feel better. "Guess no one ever showed you how to play football."

It was the best he could do, but even as an eight-year-old, I knew better. Plenty of guys could play without the benefit of a father's backyard coaching. It wasn't the fact that I'd never be a good athlete that I hated as much as I hated being afraid of sports: the collisions, the speed, the energy, the emotion.

"Not really," I said wanting to change the subject. "We still gonna go see *Empire Strikes Back*?"

My fat lip throbbed. I was trying not to drip blood on his seats.

"Naw," he said. "I got an idea."

That was the first time we went to the Cowboys' training facility, but thereafter it replaced all the fun and games that had filled our schedule. At first I hated it, though I never said a word to Preston. It was hard work. He got the trainers to find gym shorts my size, and they special-ordered a pair of shoes for me. It was cool seeing some of the other Cowboy players push themselves through off-season workouts, but Preston wasn't all that social at the training facility. He was down to business, and business was making an athlete out of me. He didn't start slow: an hour of agility drills—high-stepping through tires and ropes, weaving around cones, backpedaling at crazy angles. He made me hold a football the whole time. Take it home with me at night. Sleep with it.

Preston always held a stopwatch and timed everything we did, occasionally giving me updates. "Cut a second off your tire time," he'd say.

I charted my progress at home and imagined myself on a collector card.

I loved hanging out with Preston, but I didn't quit

dreading the workouts until one day I realized I wasn't falling down as much anymore. I wasn't fast by Oak Cliff standards, and he hadn't dared throw me a pass, but I was getting there. I began secretly wishing someone would set up tires and ropes in the hallways at school, make us backpedal to class. On my way to school I would carioca down the lines in the streets — running sideways, lead leg out, back leg over, lead leg out, back leg under. I did it like Preston showed me, head swiveling, eyes scanning the sky, ready to pull down an INT and take it the other way for six.

"Make 'em pay," Preston would say. "If they don't respect you, make 'em pay."

He started me on weights and distance running. I attacked both disciplines. I didn't have to be such a good athlete. All I had to do was ignore the pain, and I'd been practicing that my whole life. Preston would lift and jog right next to me and ask me what I'd do with all my money when I was a pro athlete. I was always breathing too hard to answer, but I started making a list in my head: a house for Momma, cereal that came in boxes instead of plastic sacks, my own Pizza Hut franchise. Preston was always going on about getting himself a deep-sea fishing boat. He kept stacks of brochures in his glove compartment. He'd have me get them out and tell him which I liked best. I put a deep-sea fishing boat on my list. For Preston, if he didn't have one by then. I figured it was the least I could do.

After our first month, Preston made a little poster

and told me to hang it in my room next to my mirror.

GOALS

40-yard dash — 6.0 seconds

Bench press — your weight

Mile run — 6 minutes

Preston led me to his locker. He held out one of his real game jerseys. It was huge, blue and silver — beautiful. I reached out and touched the heavy mesh.

"It's yours when you reach your goals," he promised.

I pictured myself walking down the halls at school in that jersey. My knees got weak.

The mile time was cake. I came home and put a line through it. The bench press took me a couple months. Another line. The first time Preston timed me in the 40, I clocked a 6.6. I had it down to a 6.2, but I wasn't getting any faster than that. You'd think that with all of the working out, I would've been anxious to start playing real football, but I wasn't. I was still afraid. The day Preston came out of the equipment room carrying that huge Wilson, I wanted to disappear. Preston took me out to the AstroTurf practice field. He positioned me on the twenty yard line, planted himself on the twenty-five, and tossed me the ball, softly. I wasn't afraid of it, but it bounced off my chest and fell to the ground nonetheless. Preston was close enough to me that he could talk without raising his voice.

"Catch with your hands, little man," he said.

I threw the ball back to him.

"With your hands," he repeated. "Look here."

Preston tucked the ball between his knees, held his hands out, and spread his fingers. His thumb and index fingers touched, creating a natural aperture.

"What's that hole look like, little man?"

"I don't know."

"The shape . . . "

"A diamond?"

Preston chuckled.

"That ain't what my coaches called it, but you're young still," Preston said. "All right, when the ball comes, I want you to watch it all the way in through that . . . diamond. Ready?"

I nodded, and Preston tossed a soft spiral toward me. I made the diamond with my fingers and watched the ball approach through the hole. At the last minute, though, I snapped my eyes shut, tried to close my fingers too soon, and ended up getting my pinky jammed as a result.

I couldn't catch a soft toss from five yards away. I went home that day more beaten than I'd been since we started.

The next time we went ou to the practice field, it was with a Nerf ball. I was much better at keeping my eyes open with the soft foam zipping in at me. I caught most of them. Preston kept trying to get me to catch ten in a row, but he wouldn't count any that I trapped against my chest. He'd only count the ones I caught away from my body with my hands. He'd always intentionally throw a couple bad ones to test me. It took me an hour and a half, but when I finally got ten in a row, Preston called it a day.

And that's how it went for the next few weeks: We'd work out first, then after I caught ten in a row, we'd "take it to the house." Every week he'd back up another three yards, but when he got to twenty yards he stopped. For one thing, I couldn't throw the ball back any farther than that. In the meantime, I got my 40 down to a 6.1—a tenth of a second from owning that jersey. The week after I caught my ten at twenty yards, Preston brought the Wilson back out. The first pass he threw, I was blinking so fast that it was like trying to catch with a disco light flashing. The ball smacked me in the nose, but this time I didn't let Preston know it hurt. I hurled the ball back. He caught it on one hop.

He reached into a gym bag and pulled out the sort of goggles Kareem Abdul-Jabbar wore.

"Put these on," he said.

I caught the next eight he threw me before I dropped a bullet that came in at knee level. The next week we started running pass routes: posts, curls, flags, down and outs, down and ins. I couldn't wait for our workouts after that. Preston started calling me Bug, because of the way I looked in the goggles.

"Down and out, Bug."

"Juke the safety, Bug."

"Sand wedge, Bug."

That was when he had me caddie for him in a golf tournament for charity that one of the other Cowboy players organized. I'd never been on a golf course before. I'd only seen them on TV. They look nicer in person. All that grass, clipped and perfect. Trees and streams. White sand in perfect dunes. Other Cowboys had their sons carrying their clubs. Preston had me. A TV reporter interviewed Preston, and he made them get me in the shot. His arm draped across my shoulder. On the way home we stopped at Preston's house. I couldn't believe he lived there himself. You could've fit three or four of our houses in his. It had a four-car garage. A pool with a slide. A big-screen TV. There was a room with nothing but trophies, game balls, and framed magazines with Preston on the cover.

I found out the next day at school that a few of the guys had seen me on TV. Instead of being impressed, it made them hate me more. They couldn't get over how Preston Moncrief was friends with a nothing like me. At recess a couple of them asked if I wanted to play football. The same guys played every day. Not even two-below; they played tackle on the solidly packed dirt of the playground. I'd always been safe before. They knew I didn't play; they never asked. Now they had something to prove. I didn't deserve to be friends with a Dallas Cowboy. I should be skipping rope with the girls.

I couldn't back out, but I needed my goggles. I couldn't catch without my goggles. I'd blink. Then again, they'd probably never throw to me. Why throw to me when Stephawn Coleman was on the same field? I said yeah, then stretched out my legs like Preston taught me. That made a few of them laugh.

The game started, and for the first eight or nine plays I didn't have much to do. I ran down and outs when we had the ball, and covered their slowest, worst player when they had the ball. The other team wasn't even bothering to cover me. It didn't matter. I didn't even mention it. No one was going to throw me the ball. Fine with me. I found I was enjoying the running around. Just feeling a part of the game, even if it was a small part.

The next play I got more involved. James Burleson, the other team's best player, caught a pass over the middle. Stephawn was supposed to be covering him, but he'd gotten faked out. I had an angle on James, coming in from his blind side. I didn't even stop and think. There wasn't time. I took three steps and dove. My shoulder slammed into his knee, and he fell hard, though my head cushioned the blow for him. I was too dizzy to stand all the way up. I climbed to one knee, and was vaguely aware of teammates slapping me on the back.

I got in on a couple more tackles and one pass was thrown to me, but it was way over my head, so I didn't even get my hand on it. The first bell rang ending recess, but the score was tied and the other team had gotten the ball first, so we kept playing. I kept running my down and outs. On fourth down, I looked back after making my cut and saw our quarterback scrambling. I was running out of field, so I cut up the sideline toward the end zone. I looked back again and saw the strangest thing. The football was on its way.

It was coming to me if I just kept running. I brought my hands up, formed my diamond, framed the ball with it.

You don't need goggles if you just catch it.

The ball was like a jet landing on an aircraft carrier, skidding and stopping, still inches from my face. I squeezed, tucked, imagined ropes, and high-stepped across the goal line. I got tackled, but it was by my own teammates who had sprinted up behind me to celebrate.

I couldn't concentrate the rest of the school day; I was so anxious for it to end. It was Tuesday, and that meant Preston would be picking me up. I couldn't wait to tell him, couldn't wait to run another 40. Today was the day. Six-flat. Bet on it. I'd be wearing that jersey to school tomorrow, and no one would make fun of me for it. Preston was my best friend, my big brother. I wanted to tell him that, but after school he didn't show.

At first I thought I had the days wrong, but I got home, checked, and found out I didn't. Something had probably come up. I blew it off until Thursday, but he didn't show up then either. I tried calling him from home. I left a message on his machine. I called the Cowboys' practice facility, but they treated me like I was just some stupid kid. School ended a couple weeks later, and I still hadn't heard from Preston. I kept asking Momma what had happened. She asked me if I wanted to sign up for a new Big Brother. I yelled at her that I already had one. For some reason

I blamed it on her. I thought maybe Preston had been traded, but when it was time for training camp, I saw him interviewed on TV talking about the chances for the next season.

The reporter asked him a question about his "troubled off-season."

Preston said that he had put that behind him. "Two hundred hours of community service and you can bet you'll learn your lesson," he said.

I think I was fifteen or sixteen before I really understood what that meant.

So now I'm holding nine folders. I'll start the interviews tonight. I'm anxious to get this assignment over with. Just leafing through these volunteers' evaluation sheets, I can already see they gave the program a big thumbs up. Telling their teachers what they wanted to hear. There's a great tradition of that. Maybe I'll do the same, but you know, before Preston Moncrief I didn't know shacks from mansions, so excuse me if I don't join the Hallelujah Chorus over three hundred high school kids set loose on the community, blindly colliding, if only momentarily, with real people living real lives. Those lives keep going long after the kids have reduced them to a line on a college application.

Loss of Pet

"I could kill an Arab."

Andrew is notoriously dramatic, so it doesn't surprise me when this proclamation is delivered without a segue. The two of us hadn't spoken for the previous fifteen minutes. We'd just been reading. Andrew is working on *The Stranger*, the Camus book I told him about. That's what most of this job is, really. Reading. Makes sense. We work at the library. But we're *clerks*. Not librarians. If we were librarians, we might actually have to lift a finger every now and then. Locate arcane shit. They, the public *they*, are always calling in to find the most random info: the original copyright date on *The Old Man and the Sea*, the name of the third witch in *Macbeth*. When we get a call like that, Andrew and I just hand the phone off to one of the librarians. They're making the big money. We're volunteers. Slave labor, really. We're here because Lee High requires two hundred hours of community service for graduation. We spent weeks scrutinizing the list of homeless shelters, crisis hot lines, and hospital possiblities, then Andrew and I penciled in "public library" as our number one choice. Neither of us are what you call people people. In fact, I'm one of two people Andrew says he can tolerate. I used to think the other was his boyfriend, but he says he can't stand him either.

"Which Arab?" I say.

"Any Arab," says Andrew. "I'm not saying I'm going to kill the next Arab I meet, but if I happened to kill one. Well, I'd just go on living."

"You'd head up to the Electric Lounge. Catch the next Wannabes show?"

"Mosh. Sing along. Wouldn't bother me a bit. I'm not saying I'd be happy about it. Or proud. But I'd feel the same about anyone. Any victim, that is. Chinese. Canadian. Even less if they were from Fort Worth."

"What about a kid?" I say. "Does icing a Cub Scout merit any guilt?"

Andrew has to think about this. He aligns his index finger with his nose and closes his eyes. He speaks without opening them.

"Yeah. I'd feel bad about a kid. Kids are still innocent. Most of them anyway. I think high school is about the cutoff. I don't think anyone's guiltless after that."

"Including me? Including *you*?"

"Especially me," he says. "You, Fiona? I would be sad about you, but only because you're maybe the only person I know not infected by The Rot."

The Rot.

That's what Andrew and I call it. It's everywhere. It's the sorority girl who parks in the handicapped zone because she's still got the permit they gave her when she broke her leg jet skiing. It's the politician who promises to restore family values. It's the people throwing "Welcome Home" parties for that boxer who raped a girl. It's television. It's every U2 album after *War*. It's the women who come in here with black eyes and check out romance novels. It's sex in general. It's the jocks at school who whistle at Andrew when he walks down the hall, or the dance team girls who ask me whether I've ever seen the sun. That's The Rot.

The phone rings, and Andrew and I look at each other. We both hate answering the phone. We roshambo. He rocks. I scissor. I pick it up.

"Deerfield Public Library," I drone.

But no one responds. I start to hang up, but just as I'm bringing the receiver away from my ear, I hear a voice.

"Excuse me?"

Even with the receiver pressed back against my ear, the voice is thin and soft. "Is there a loss of pet meeting there tonight?"

"A loss of what?" I say, sure I heard her wrong.

"Pet." This time there's no mistaking the word.

"Just a minute," I barely get the hold button pushed before I burst out laughing.

"God, Fiona." Andrew cringes. He hates loud noises.

"Some chick wants to know if there's a loss of pet meeting here tonight."

Andrew's giggle tapers off quickly. "You know what? I think I saw something about that on the calendar."

"Tell me you're joking."

He digs through the pile of announcements on his desk.

"Eight P.M., LBJ Room," he says, shaking his head in disbelief.

"You do it," I say, pushing the phone toward him. "I won't be able to tell her without laughing in her face."

"You're wicked," he says, but his expression indicates he approves. He takes the phone from my hand and punches the hold button. "Eight P.M., LBJ Room." Andrew pauses. I'm biting my index finger to keep from flying into hysterics. "I'm sorry, ma'am. I don't know if there'll be a slide projector."

That does it. I scream. Andrew slams down the phone.

"Jesus, Fiona. She heard that. You sounded like a hyena."

"Have you ever heard a hyena, Andrew?"

"I had a hyena once," Andrew says. He sighs. "But I must've misplaced him."

We both crack up. The woman Andrew calls "The Bun" despite the fact that her hair is stylishly bobbed sticks her head out of the office.

"Cool it," says The Bun.

"*Cool it*," Andrew mimics when The Bun is no

longer visible. "Aren't we modern."

"I don't get it," I say. "There's so much shit in the world. I mean, look at Bosnia, or Rwanda, or Ethiopia. Tens of thousands of people dying, but tonight in Deerfield, a group of people are gathering to try to get over Spot getting sent to the great back-yard in the sky. I wonder if they've ever heard the phrase *get a life*."

"You go, girl," says Andrew.

"I'm sorry, Andrew, but I don't believe in any of it."

"Dead pets? You think they're really still alive?"

"No, smart ass—Self-help. Analysis. Therapy. Support groups. Pop psychology. Sharing. Group hugs. I'm okay, you're okay. It's all bullshit."

"Why don't you point that out to the group tonight?"

"What do you mean?"

"I mean," he says, "that you promised The Bun you'd work late tonight if she let you off last weekend to go camping with your family."

"Shit."

"Your mom must have been a cruise director in a former life," says Andrew. It's one of his favorite top-ics—my mom's quality-time addiction. Frankly, her gusto is wearing.

"The family that bowls together . . . " I say.

The news that I have to work late puts me in a foul mood for the next two hours. I don't shelve a thing. Neither does Andrew, but he never does. He reads me a magazine quiz devised to tell me how my per-ception of my body affects my self-image.

"I'm fat; therefore I am," I say.

"You're so *not* fat, Fiona. You know how you should know?"

I shake my head no.

"Because I'd tell you if you were."

There's actually some truth in that. He would.

Andrew leaves at six, blowing me a kiss and telling me not to work too hard. By seven I've reshelved everything in the return bin. Just before eight o'clock, I'm cutting out dinosaur-shaped badges—rewards for our "Kids Read" program—when the former pet owners start shuffling into the nearly deserted branch. I spot them right off. The woman have red rings around their eyes, and the men seem to walk without strength—each step quite possibly their last. They all look like they've experienced their loss within the past twenty minutes.

The sight of our next patron causes me to impale myself with the scissors. I simply can't believe it. Tamara Reynolds. Lee High's former She-Queen of Step Aerobics, Patron Saint of Tanning Salons, Pool Party Goddess. I would be surprised enough if she were here simply returning a book—it would imply she had read one—but what's she's carrying in her hands, it's too good to be true.

It's a carousel . . . for slides.

Tamara scans the library, regally, deftly avoiding eye contact with me, then joins the procession into the meeting room that doubles as our reference room. I'm on the phone in an instant, dialing Andrew's pager number. I have an overwhelming desire to share this development.

The group has been in the LBJ Room for ten minutes when I'm approached by The Bun. She tells me that she needs—right, she *needs*—a box full of microfiche refiled.

"They're using the reference room," I mention.

"Well, be very quiet while you're in there," she reponds.

So I open the one giant door in the front of the reference room with whatever stealth I can muster. I expect people to stare up at me, but no one does. An elderly man is speaking. I duck behind the cabinets where we store our microfiche and try not to listen, but I'm only semisuccessful. He's talking about his parakeet. A bird, for chrissakes! Someone asks him what he taught the bird to say, but the man explains that parakeets don't talk.

"But they sing," I hear him say, maybe even a bit defensively. "Oh, how I miss the sound of Sweet Pea singing."

"Did you bring pictures?" someone asks.

"I did," says the old man.

I can't see over the cabinet, but I heard the mourners *oohing* and *aahing*. All I can think of is an old Monty Python skit where someone describes a dead parrot as having "beautiful plumage." "Oh, how I miss the sound of Sweet Pea singing" is even funnier. I put my hand over my mouth so no one can hear me snickering.

The next woman to speak says she ran over her own dog. This, too, strikes me as somewhat humorous. She explains that the dog was old and had been deaf for years. It was under the car when she started it, but of course, the dog couldn't hear. The woman starts choking up.

"He used to get under there all the time. I should have checked. I was just in a hurry. I should have checked."

She struggles to add that the dog, a beagle named Duffy, survived, but both his hipbones were broken and his legs were crushed.

"My husband wasn't home, and I had to take him to the vet by myself. The vet said I should put him to sleep. He said Duffy would spend the rest of his life in pain if I didn't. But Duffy was fifteen. He's a year older than my son. I wanted to call my husband, let him make the decision, but I didn't know where he was, so I had to do it. *I* had to tell the vet to put him to sleep."

The woman falls apart again, and I hear the sounds of people comforting her, telling her she made the right decision. Between sniffles, she finishes her story.

"I was right there when the vet did it. I was hugging Duffy when the injection was given to him. He just kept looking at me like he knew what was happening. He looked so sad, but there was so much trust in his eyes. He kept licking my face for as long as he could. God, you take for granted how loyal a dog is for so long, and then when you have to do something like that . . . First I run over him, then I have him put to sleep."

This time when the sobbing starts, it's not just from the woman telling the story. Why is The Bun making me do this? I can't alphabetize with this going on around me. Besides, no one looks anything up on microfiche. Meanwhile, the stories continue. I keep expecting someone to suggest strategies for healing or methods of coping, but no one does. They just talk about their pets and what they've meant to them.

One man tells the group that his wife asked him why he just couldn't get a new cat when he couldn't get over the loss of his former one.

"Can you believe some people think that way?" he asks. "Like Mimi was a shoe or a golf club—something I could just go out and replace. I love my wife, but sometimes, I just don't know."

When the lights are turned off so Tamara can show her slides, I give up any pretense of trying to work. My first thought is that this would be a good chance to escape, but I'm sort of curious about what Miss Perfect will say. From my space behind the microfiche cabinet, I'm unable to see any of the people, but I can watch the screen. The first slide that appears is of a puppy. A poodle. That figures. The dog has a tiny set of those fake reindeer horns attached to its head.

"I named him Blitzen," Tamara begins, "because I got him for Christmas when I was nine. That was my best Christmas ever, and not just because of Blitzen. My parents were still together, and they weren't fighting much. Dad got Mom a Lexus, so even if there wasn't peace on earth, there was, for once, around the house.

"Naturally it didn't last. Mom wrecked the car within a couple of months and Dad wouldn't get it fixed. Who knows what he used the insurance money for, but at least things were better for me, because I had Blitzen. I don't have any brothers or sisters, and we moved so much that my best friend was always my dog."

The slide changes. Blitzen's bigger, and he's got a his mouth clamped nearly all the way around a tennis ball. I didn't realize poodles came in this extra-large variety. Tamara continues talking with none of the verge-of-crying vibrato that made the people who went before her nearly unintelligible.

"I know some people think poodles are annoying. Everyone makes fun of them, but Blitzen was cool. He was smart. He was a great fetcher. You know how you can fake dogs out when you're throwing a ball— act like you're throwing, but keep it in your hand, and the dog goes tearing off looking all stupid. Blitzen never fell for that. He would just look at you like, 'Gimme a break.' And he was tough too. There was a German shepherd that lived next door when we were living in Atlanta, and if it got anywhere near me, Blitzen would chase it away. I never saw him run from another dog. Not once."

A new picture appears on the screen. This one is of Blitzen and a teenaged Tamara. Tamara's holding a camera, and it takes me a few seconds to realize that she took this photo by aiming into a mirror.

"By this time, the folks have split up and Mom's moved us to Dallas. As miserable as Mom was with Dad, she got worse, and she started taking it out on me. It seems like every day she would tell me how much prettier she was than me when she was in high school, and how she always had boyfriends—not a dog—to spend time with. She bought me these expensive clothes that she knew I'd never wear. Then when I didn't, she'd put on this major hurt-feelings act and tell me how ungrateful I was. I started staying out late. I'd go on these long walks, but I'd take Blitzen. I went into some pretty rough areas, but I always felt safe."

I find myself thinking about my cruise director mother. Could be worse, I guess. Tamara returns to her story. More pictures flash up on the screen. Blitzen taking a bath. Blitzen on a beanbag chair. Blitzen with a shoe in his mouth. Tamara returns to her story.

"One morning after one of my walks, Mom came storming into my room demanding to know where I was. I told her I was just out walking, but she didn't believe me. She called me a bunch of names and told me she knew I was slutting around. I told her 'like mother like daughter,' and she went ballistic. She reached out to slap me, but Blitzen was in the room, and out of nowhere there came this growl. It was the first time I had ever heard him growl at a person.

"Mom froze. Then she said, 'Get your dog in the car. We're taking him to the pound.'

"'Oh no we're not,' I said. And I was ready to fight her. Run away. Anything."

I draw in my breath thinking I know where the story is heading. Tamara continues.

"Then Mom started crying. I'm sure she was probably drunk, and she goes, 'You love that dog more than you love me.'

"So I told her she was right."

She changes slides. This one shows Blitzen lying across what I assume is Tamara's bed. None of the personal effects I would have imagined in Tamara Reynolds's boudoir appear in the picture. No fluffy pillows. No long-withered mums. No framed pictures of beefy, clean-cut boys. Nothing I can use to shut this out.

"Mom and I don't speak much after that. She gets remarried to someone she meets waiting in a line at Neiman Marcus, and we move down to Deerfield. I'm just happy that the new guy has a big yard. For a while things are decent enough. I'm not making many friends, but I don't really try very hard anymore. Then Mom's husband starts doing weird things. He walks into the bathroom without knocking when I'm in there, or I find him sitting around the living room with his robe wide open. When it happens, he acts embarrassed and says something about not being used to having women around. Then he starts touching me, so I decide to tell Mom. That's when she slapped me and told me I was making it up because I hated her."

The projector advances, but Tamara's out of slides and the screen is left white. She continues telling her story as her shadow, a perfect female silhouette, passes through the light.

"I start talking to the few friends I have about staying with them, just for a little while. I figure if I can line up places to crash, a week here, a week there, I can avoid going home ever again. I just had to make it through graduation. But it's one thing to ask if *you* can sleep over for a week. Start asking for lodging for both you *and* your dog—you find out who your real friends are.

"The same day that my friend Mindy tells me Blitzen and I can stay with her until graduation, they found my mom in her car in the garage. She'd run a hose from the exhaust pipe into the back window."

The room is silent as Tamara's stoicism begins to fail her. She sniffles. The first sobs sound choked back, but then she wails. I've never heard anybody cry like this. I'm sure they can hear her out on the floor. I know she must blame herself for telling her mother she loves her dog more, maybe even for telling her mom about the husband. I want somebody to make her stop crying, tell her it isn't her fault, hold her. I feel myself rising to do the job myself, but when Tamara speaks again, I sink back to the floor.

"That bitch put Blitzen in the car with her."

Tamara sobs some more, but it's apparent she's reached the part of the story she wants to tell.

"I've never cried for Blitzen. That's who I'm crying for now. When it happened, I wouldn't let myself. I told myself my mother was dead and that losing my dog shouldn't be important to me. I thought that if I told anyone that I missed Blitzen, they'd think I was horrible or sick. When people talked to me after that, no one ever even mentioned him. I know where my mom is buried. I never got to see Blitzen again. I wanted to find people who could understand. It's been two years now. I've never told anyone. I miss him. He was my best friend."

I don't know what goes on after that on the other side of the cabinets. I hear a few kind words. I imagine a lot of hugging. I stay hidden until I'm sure everyone's gone. Then I pick myself up, feeling clammy and drained. As I exit the reference room, the phone on my desk rings. There's nobody to roshambo with, so I pick it up.

"You paged?" says Andrew, giggling like he does when he's high.

"I wanted to know where the Liquid Paper was, but I found it."

"If I had known it was that important, I would have sent Keanu home sooner," he says, employing his famous sarcasm. "So what were the pet mourners like? Spooky?"

"Yeah," I say, attempting to chuckle.

"Part of The Rot, huh?" he says.

I check the clock hanging above Andrew's desk, relieved that it reads ten o'clock—closing time. In the glass, I catch my reflection.

"Well?" Andrew says impatiently.

"The list keeps getting longer," I tell him.

Box Nine

Look at all this shit. Ain't nothin' I'd stick in my own mouth. Nonperishable charity. Foodstuff can-me-downs. Creamed corn . . . *right*. And look at them, all fussing over it. Dividing it up like it's some feast fit for a king. Apricots in heavy syrup? *Put those in box three.* Minute Rice? *Box six ain't got nothing starchy.*

I stand back and watch them go at it. I'm just cozed being out of class.

"Teesha, give me a hand here," hollers Mr. Lansing, the food drive committee sponsor.

So I clap.

And look *real* bored.

He goes, "I still haven't signed your community service completion form."

The way he says it—it's like he thinks I'm gonna pucker up and kiss his butt right there. Think again, fat man. I wanna tell him what he can do with his

John Hancock, but Robert E. Lee High School don't let you walk the stage at graduation without that community service form. Walking the stage—that's real important to Gramma, so I sort of stroll over to the van, chompin' my Bubblicious. He's waiting there, holding onto box nine.

"Well?" I say.

Lansing's breathing hard. The box he's holding is cram packed.

He's all, "Mind opening the door? If you're not *indisposed*."

So I do. The rest of the do-good posse follows Lansing with the food. Boxes six, seven, eight, and nine wind up in the van. Boxes one through five get loaded on the short bus—the one that brings the retarded kids to school. Lansing makes me ride in the van with him. Fine with me. We got one less box to deliver.

We been priming for this day for a long time. Ever since the first week of school. But that's one reason I signed up for food drive. Gets over with by Thanksgiving. Me? I did my part. Sort of. I worked the door at *Tom Jones*. Three cans got you in. Ten cans got you close enough so you could actually hear the actors' fake accents. I checked out a bit of it. One brotha in the whole show, and guess what? He played the highway robber. Don't *even* get me started.

The worst part of being on the committee was the businesses. We had to ask five restaurants or grocery stores to donate food. Mr. Lansing lined up the turkeys and hams from H.E.B. All the rest was up for grabs. If you were smart, you did it right away, but I put it off until there was nothing left but Sac-N-Pacs. I didn't like the whole idea. It was like begging, and Gramma didn't raise no beggars. Mr. Lansing said you had to ask five businesses. He didn't say you had to get any of them to say yes. Good thing, 'cuz I went oh for five.

After the boxes get loaded, I work my way to the backseat of the van and flop my legs across it so no one even thinks to sit next to me. Like I'm gonna have that problem. It's just that, when you got three little wanna-be gangsta brothers, you never get a seat to yourself. Mr. Lansing climbs in the driver's seat, and the others—Chip, Daphne, Lyle—fight over shotgun. Like we're going to Six Flags or something.

Lansing goes, "All aboard."

What is it with teachers?

Tomorrow's Thanksgiving. We're taking all this food to "the needy." People on the committee always using those words . . . "the needy." They get a list every year from the Deerfield Council of Churches. Bet you the other three food drivers in this here van all live in fancy subdivisions west of 35 with names like "Country Estates," or "Spicewood Gardens" or "River Oaks." Tomorrow they'll sit around their dining room tables and give thanks and talk about how they "fed the needy" the day before. But you know what? None of 'em'll eat better than me. They ain't got my gramma.

Don't get me wrong. My gramma ain't one of those old ladies who got nothing better to do than kiss your cheek and bake you cookies. First off, she ain't that old. Second, she works full time hostess-ing at the Kettle. Lots of night shifts. So me and the little Tupacs, we take care of ourselves. Lots of macaroni. Lots of peanut butter. Momma liked to cook some, but she headed up to Michigan looking for work last spring. She's always calling to check up on us, but never when I'm home. Gramma says she keeps making noises about flying back down to see me walk.

Anyways.

Thanksgiving Gramma does right. Big ol' ham. Casserole. Cornbread. Okra. Sweet potatoes. Damn, just thinking about it is making me hungry.

Our first stop is some kinda aquamarine blue shack in Little Matamoros. Chip, who I guess won the race for shotgun, swear-to-God *sprints* to the back door of the van and lifts out box six.

Mr. Lansing checks his list and goes, "Escobar. This is it."

There's a chain-link fence all around the tiny dirt yard, and a skinny dog is yappin' at us and turnin' circles. Mr. Lansing opens the gate and keeps say-ing, "Good boy" to the dog. We have to watch out for toy cars and dog shit in the yard. I can't keep from stomping on a couple half-buried army men.

Mr. Lansing makes us all get in a little huddle on the porch before he'll knock on the door. This short, round Mexican lady opens it up happy as can be — like us standin' here was normal. If I found a bunch of high school kids on my porch, I'd shoot first, dispose of the bodies later, but she waves us in. Chip carries box six up on his shoulder so proud, like he's some Apache returning with enough buffalo to get the tribe through the winter. We walk into the kitchen, passing along the way a man on a couch puffing a cigarette. At first I think he must be watching television, he's so set on ignoring us, but I look to where his eyes are pointing and all that's there is a Texas Rangers poster. We're just invisible to him. Once we get in the kitchen, Chip sets the food on the table.

Mr. Lansing looks at the lady, serious as a preacher, and goes, "The students of Robert E. Lee High School would like to present you this food in hopes that you'll have a happy and bountiful Thanksgiving."

The round Mexican lady just keeps noddin' at Mr. Lansing and smiling. I think I'm the first to figure it out. She don't speak English. That leaves all us standing around looking stupid. I don't know what we're waiting for. It's like Chip and Mr. Lansing are expecting medals or something.

I'm all, "One down. Three to go." No one's movin', so I tack on, "Shotgun."

That sets things in motion.

We deliver box seven just a few blocks away. On

the drive over, there's a bunch of talking.

Chip goes, "Did you see the size of that roach? I thought it was gonna carry the turkey away."

When he's through laughing, Lyle puts in his cent's worth. "And what was the deal with the corpse in the living room? It's like, 'Hello, señor. We're helping you out. You might want to get up and thank us.'"

Then Daphne. "And how can he afford cigarettes if they don't have enough money for food?"

At the De La Rosas' the old lady we're giving the food to bursts out crying as she starts pulling cans of spinach out of the box. She's trying to hug every one of us, but I keep moving around so she misses me. Mrs. De La Rosa pulls a pitcher out of the fridge and pours everyone a full 7-Eleven Dallas Cowboys Collector's Cup of lemonade. I notice that Chip doesn't drink from his. Then there's more hugging before we're able to get out the door.

On the way to drop off box eight, Lyle goes, "Now that was how it's supposed to work. That was some real appreciation."

I say, "I don't know how she can afford to give lemonade away when they don't have enough money for food." I say it like a real bitch, but no one gets it.

Daphne looks all worried and goes, "Maybe we shoulda told her we weren't thirsty." In the back of the van, I point an imaginary gun at her ponytail and pull the trigger.

Box eight goes to someone I know. Rachelle Warner. She goes to our church. She ain't tons older than me. I'm not sure she's even twenty yet, but she's already got three kids. There's pictures of them all over the house. Happy poses with little footballs and stuffed bears. The pictures make me a little jealous. So does her having her own half a duplex. She keeps it real clean. I would too. On her refrigerator there's a finger painting one of her babies done in church day care. I know that's where 'cuz of the little lamb stamp the teacher's stuck on it. I've seen plenty of them lamb stamps in my lifetime.

Rachelle acts thankful for the food and all, but there's crying coming from the bedroom, so we clear out of there pretty quick. As we're heading out the door, Rachelle says she'll see me Sunday.

The group starts up with all their noise when we get back in the van.

Chip goes first. "People shouldn't have babies if they can't afford to feed them."

"I heard all three babies have different fathers," says Lyle.

I'm in the back with my eyes closed trying to keep from hearing all this.

"How'd you like the towels she was using for curtains?" laughs Daphne.

And they go on.

I drift off wondering what made segregated schools such a bad thing. I feel the van stop and I hear Mr. Lansing. "Walker. This is it."

Walker . . . ? That's my gramma's name.

I open my eyes, and there's my house. I feel like I'm looking at it for the first time. There's the tin roof. And the paint peeling off the sides. And the Granada on blocks.

This time Lyle beats Chip to the back of the van. He grabs box nine. I look over the seat and check out what's inside it. Stringed beans, mushroom soup, crunchy fried onions. Gramma'll make her casserole with those. The Ro-tel tomatoes she'll dump in with the canned okra. There's the Bacos for the cornbread. And the ham. We been eating like this for years.

Mr. Lansing goes, "Teesha, come on."

So I do.

We huddle up, then knock. Gramma opens the door. I see her see me, but she doesn't say a thing. So I don't either. We go inside, and all I can think about is how funky it smells. It started stinking a couple weeks ago. It got so bad, we sent Chuckie under the house. He found a dead snake and pulled it out, but the house still ain't smelling right. Gramma's acting nice to everyone. She's not shedding tears or giving us anything to drink, but she smiles and says thank you to everyone. It's all I can do to keep from pushing people out the door.

Finally Mr. Lansing says we should be going.

On the van ride back to school, Chip smiles and goes, "Hey Teesha, that little girl in the picture in the hallway sure looked like you."

"We all look alike," I say all sarcastic.

"That's not what I—"

I'm still facing out the window when I cut him off. "Anyone else think it stunk in there?"

Cheatin' Heart

Cole brings the faders on the soundboard down gradually. As the volume fades, he presses play on the tape machine. His recorded voice fills the sound booth.

"Ah, tell us about it Hank. Now, there's a man who knew a thing or two about loneliness. I know how he feels. This is Cole Clay Ellum...all by his lonesome."

But he's not by his lonesome. I'm here. It's three in the morning, and I wish I weren't, but Cole would be the first to tell you that if wishes and buts were candy and nuts, we'd all have fat asses. Cole's almost a poet.

"All righty, Sid Vicious," Cole says as he starts buttoning up a freshly starched French flag-looking button down, "you know what to do?"

We've been over this before, but I repeat his instructions. "Run a PSA after 'All My Exes.' Flip the tape. Press play."

Cole grins. "Whoever said you was dimmer'n a trucker's wife?"

"You did. About an hour ago."

"But who's keepin' score?" Clay says. "As far as punk rock listenin', skateboard ridin', seal-savin' dope-heads, I think you're aces . . . the frostiest of the flakes."

"Gosh, thanks," I say.

Cole slaps on more Brut than a lodgeful of Shriners.

"What's special about tonight?" I ask. "Ladies' night at the Easy Shitkicker? Quarter tequila for whoever can name two Billy Ray Cyrus songs?"

"Laugh all you want, Miles. Half hour from now one of us'll be churnin' torso butter; one of us'll be holdin' a Shania Twain poster one-handed in the little boys' room. Care to make any wagers?"

I don't say anything, so Cole lays in some more.

"Haven't seen that sweet thing comin' to pick you up for school lately. Mandy? Marcia?"

"Macy."

"She nasty? Maybe I'll give her a call myself."

I still don't say anything, hoping he'll get off this.

"She looked nasty to me. Sometimes you can just tell. Punk rock girl like that. Y'all musta been bumpin' uglies. Maybe that's how come you been so grumpy lately. She dust you?"

Cole doesn't even notice me balling up my fist. Probably wouldn't care if he did. Probably just laugh, but he's entered a universe of his own now—Hair World. A place where follicle management is offered as a graduate-level course. Working with the reflection provided by the glass of the studio booth, he begins to, strand by strand, transform himself into Marshal Dillon. The guy's a dick. Normally, though, I just deal with his shit. Talking about Macy, though—that's crossing a line. We broke up a month ago after a big fight, though it didn't start off as a fight. I was just giving her a hard time about Tom Sawyering this sophomore girl into doing her science project for her. I cracked some joke about how Macy likes to push everyone around.

"Guess that's why I date you," she said.

But *she* wasn't joking.

So I'm flying solo now. I usually don't dwell on it up here at K.I. "Yippee" I.I., the only radio station in Deerfield, hometown of George Strait. I didn't know this fact until I came to work here. Apparently we were the first radio station in America to ever broadcast one of his songs. Twenty years later we're still advertising that fact in promos.

"You're listenin' to K.I."Yippee"I.I. Where George got his start."

Oh yeah. Four hundred watts of pure A.M. broadcasting muscle. We pushed him into the big time, all right. Our forty loyal listeners heard the demo. And they told two friends. And so on, and so on. K.I.I.I., or "K-Yip" as all my friends call it, starts to lose signal about halfway to Austin. I could point speakers out my bedroom window and you could hear them pretty near that far. Cowboys at school listen to it. Jocks somtimes, too, since they broadcast the Rebel games every Friday night. Nobody I hang with ever listens to it unless it's to prank call "The Honey Show." "The Honey Show" *is* pretty popular. It's 9 P.M. to 11 P.M. on Wednesday nights when nobody has anything else to do anyway.

Barb Ann "Honey" Jessup is the president of the local Daughters of the Confederacy, which, as far as I can tell, is a group that has nothing to do with the Civil War. I think it's just a name meant to keep the group "lily" as the locals say in polite company. One of the assumed duties of the Daughters is watchdogging our "community standards." They kept Prince and Metallica records out of the local Hastings and Wal-Mart. They bullied our Junior Miss into giving up her crown after she got knocked up. When the Lee High choir and drama departments teamed up to do *Jesus Christ Superstar* a couple of years ago, Honey wrote a letter to the editor of the *Deerfield Herald* asking why our youngsters were never allowed to do wholesome shows like *Bye Bye Birdie* or *Grease*.

"Which wholesome parts of *Grease* would she be talking about?" asked Winslow Kupp, my best friend and lead guitarist for LouseTrap—a band we formed last year. "Is it in 'Greased Lighting' when Danny remarks that 'the chicks'll cream,' or is it where he refers to the automobile in question as a 'real pussy wagon.'"

"I think she's speaking thematically," I said.

"And what would you say the theme is?"

I thought about it for a minute. "That if you want to keep your boyfriend, you best be willing to give it up."

"Here here," he said tapping his fist on my dashboard. "Now *there's* a valuable lesson for the youth of America."

Anyway, the Honey Show is a standard call-in. She listens to the problems of teens in the community and offers one of three useless solutions: *just say no, pray,* or my favorite, *tell your parents how you feel.* At first she had trouble getting any callers. I mean, this isn't a huge town. Everyone knows everyone. But I think it was Damien Collier, the yearbook editor, who turned it into a hit with his first prank call. He got on and claimed his name was Dick. Honey asked him what his problem was. He said he was "hurtin' . . . hurtin' real bad." After that, Hurtin' Dick would call in every week with a new life-or-death problem. He's been abused, suicidal, on crack, and I believe the only male bulimic in Texas. It's sort of a contest now among Lee students—seeing who can invent the most harrowing teen soap opera. It's priceless entertainment, but it's got the village elders a little jumpy.

I got lucky notching my community service hours through this job. They have this Career Opportunity Day every year where they pair you up with someone in the community who does what you want to do. They had me follow Bud Daley around for an afternoon since I want to work in radio someday—maybe as a jock for The Edge in Dallas or KROQ in Los Angeles, or even better, programming one of the big alternative stations somewhere in a top ten market. That's a ways off. In the meantime, Mr. Daley fixed it so I could get credit for recording public service announcements two nights a week at K-Yip. The hours suck. Two to seven in the morning. It's the only time the second booth's free for me to record. Not that I get to spend that much time in there. Cole Clay Ellum, the late night deejay, treats me like his personal slave.

I watch him make a final coif adjustment, licking down an errant sideburn curley-Q. Then comes my favorite part. He picks up his Stetson and smashes it down on his head. Go figure.

Cole scribbles something down on a little yellow Post-it and sticks it to the microphone.

"That's my pager number. In case of emergency," he says. "That's emergency with a capital *emerge*. Catch my drift, Milesy Boy?"

"Not really."

"Guess you wouldn't. Just don't call less you hafta. I promised Tennessee I'd take him to the rodeo."

"Tennessee?"

Cole grabs hold of his crotch.

"Tennessee—long name, ain't it?"

The dude is seriously proud of himself for that one. I'm anxious for him to leave, but at the same time, the prospect of being up here by myself scares me a bit.

"I'm not so sure this is a real good idea," I say.

"So?" he answers. "You're an intern. Do you know what that means in radio land? It means that if we run outta toilet paper, we use you."

I open my mouth to tell where to get off, but he just keeps going. "Intern. Definition. I'm king shit now. You do what you're told. You'll get to be king shit—*in turn*. Copacetic?"

Cole faces the window to tighten his bolo. His recorded voice introduces another song as the real thing gives me final orders.

"Now I want them CDs back in the cases. Alphamatize 'em. I'll be in at six forty-five before Buck gets in for the mornin' show."

I glance down at the assorted CDs spread out around the booth.

"Sid," Cole says, "in the immortal words of Patsy Cline . . . stay the hell up."

He points his finger at me and does a double tooth suck, and he's out the door.

I *alphamatize* for the next hour and a half or so as I listen to Clay's pre-recorded show, thinking how I'd be embarrassed if I was doing the late night shift when I was thirty-something years old in a Podunk town on a gerbil-powered station. He ought to get fired for what he's doing tonight. He's supposed to be live. It's just that no one really keeps track of him at this hour of night. If you believe a word the guy says, he's off with one of his skank, Roper-wearing, big-haired kicker gals. *Man*, that guy likes to brag. I'm thinking about the time he told me about doing it in a Porta Potti at Aquafest during a Dwight Yoakam concert when I hear something that doesn't sound quite right. It's Cole's voice. It's slowing down. Jesus!

I slide my rolling chair from the CD rack to the soundboard, but by the time I get there, Cole's completely garbled. I have no idea what to do, so I sit there with a stupid look on my face and watch the play lever on the cassette deck flip up into the off position. Now nothing is coming out of the speakers. Four hundred watts of dead air fill the airwaves of Deerfield.

The microphone is hanging right down in front of my mouth. I don't want to do it, but I don't see any options. I click down the button.

"Howdy," I say. I'm afraid it comes out more like a question. My free hand is grabbing a song cartridge down from a rack. "You're listening to K.I"—I can't believe this is about to come out of my mouth—"Yippee I.I. and this has been a test of the Emergency Broadcast System. This was only a test. So don't call in or anything . . . "

" . . . y'all."

I take the first cart I get ahold of, ram it into the player, and slide the faders up on the soundboard. Willie Nelson takes over. Appropriately enough, he urges mothers not to allow their children to become cowboys. I call the number Cole left on the Post-it and punch in the request line number. It's the only phone we have access to this late at night. The phone rings almost immediately. Well, it doesn't really ring, not in the booth—a light blinks.

Thank God.

"Get back here and fix this, you—"

"What caller am I? What caller am I?" cuts in

the excited female voice on the other end.

"Excuse me?"

"For the money song!"

I glance up at the promotions bulletin board. There's a sign in red and green marker pen.

$250 MONEY SONG
"MAMAS, DON'T LET YOUR BABIES
GROW UP TO BE COWBOYS"
PLAY ONLY DURING MORNING
DRIVE TIME.
FIRST CALLER WINS.

I look down at the phone. All five buttons are lit up.

"Sorry, l'il lady. Yer caller two. Better luck next tahm."

All the calls are from money song hopefuls. I tell them all tough luck. Cole doesn't answer the page. Willie's fading. I cue Garth Brooks before clicking the microphone on.

"Stop your callin', we got us a winner. Little Winslow Kupp says he's gonna use the cash to start payin' his share of gas money when he bums rides from his buddy. Winslow—this one's for you."

Then I bring up "Friends in Low Places."

I don't speak on air for the next half hour. I just go song to song, plugging in the advertisements according to the chart next to the CD player. I page Cole again, take a request for "Devil Went Down to Georgia"—which I have to admit I kinda like—then hunt down the longest song I can find, something called "A Boy Named Sue," by Johnny Cash, punch it, and sprint downstairs to the only bathroom in the place. Cole says he just uses a soda bottle. Says it's one of the benefits of working all alone late at night. I haven't been able to drink Mountain Dew since he shared that nugget with me.

I get back up the stairs with four seconds to spare. I plug in the first thing I find. I hear the opening guitar riff of "Achy Breaky Heart."

"Kill me now," I say to no one but myself. I start singing the lyrics Winslow made up for the song. At one point LouseTrap was thinking of covering it as a joke.

"You can do this dance . . ."

". . . mindless zombies here's your chance!"

I'm hopping around the booth doing this seriously epileptic-looking two-step. I get kind of loopy up here this late at night. Sort of makes me think of Macy. Last year we all got semidrunk and showed up at one of the high school dances. You should've seen us. My hair was still purple then. Macy was all Gothed up. We tried to do the "Cotton-Eyed Joe" and ended up starting a mosh pit in the center of the gym with Winslow, Andrew, Fiona—all the usual suspects. Ended up getting kicked out. Macy got suspended for three days for flipping off the coach who did the actual tossing. That's just how she is. Ask anybody. Macy Rollins takes no shit.

"You can shake my wang . . ."

"My big ole honkin' thang."

The phone light flickers.

"K-Yip. Whassup?"

"Cole Clay Ellum! Check your microphone, you gutter-mouthed piece of white trash."

I recognize the voice. It's Honey Jessup. I glance over at the soundboard, fearing the worst. The green light is on. The slider is all the way up. I've just shared the X-rated version of Billy Ray Cyrus with everyone awake at four forty-five A.M. in Deerfield.

"Sorry, Ma'am," I say in my best Cole Clay Ellum baritone.

At five-thirty, I page Cole one more time. Then I decide I have to share this experience with somebody. Winslow has his own line, so I call him. It takes six rings for him to answer.

"This better be good," he groans.

"It's me," I say. "Turn on K-Yip."

"Why would I want to do that?"

"Just do it."

"I don't even know if this thing gets A.M."

"Trust me. It does."

I hear him fumbling around the dial.

"Twang, twang, twang," he says, mimicking the Oak Ridge Boys once he's got it tuned in. "Boy, I would have hated to miss this. Did I mention that I was having my Juliette Lewis dream?"

"Check it out," I say.

I reach over to the turntable and make like a master scratcher.

"*El . . . El-El-El-El-El-V-V-V . . . Vira.*"

Winslow's absurd cackle explodes out of the earpiece.

"I thought you'd like that," I tell him.

"What going on up there? Is Cole Lays All'em on a piss break?"

"Nope," I say. "It's just me up here. He left a tape that was supposed—wait a minute. I'm getting a call. The rat bastard's finally calling me back."

I punch the flashing button.

"Cole Clay Ellum answering service."

There's no response to that right away. When I do hear a voice, it's female. "Could I speak to my husband, please?"

Right.

"I'm sorry, ma'am. This is a radio station. You must have the wrong number."

"Just get me Cole," she says.

Oh, shit!

I start stammering. "Oh. I'm sorry. I didn't think . . . I mean . . . I never . . . He's sick, ma'am. Real sick. I'm just filling in. I think he's downstairs throwing up. Must've been something bad in the Copenhagen. Yeah, something definitely rotten in Denmark, all right."

"Look here, you lyin' sack o' shit. I'm gonna be there in thirty minutes, and if that wooden-dicked playboy ain't there, I'm gonna kick your ass first, then his."

I decide she isn't buying it.

"Uh, ma'am, I don't think—"

But she hangs up on me.

I frantically press a button on the phone and get a fresh dial tone. I punch in the first six numbers of Cole's pager number. Then I stop, my eyes locked on the cassette deck. I don't need this shit.

Twenty-seven minutes later, I'm in my Mitsubishi. K.I.I.I. is deserted and the front door is unlocked, but I don't care. I pull out of the parking lot and onto Ranch Road 12. I tune in good ol' 620 A.M. in time to hear the last chorus of "Mamas, Don't Let Your Babies Grow Up to Be Cowboys." My own voice comes out the speakers as the song fades.

"That was the K.I. 'Yippee' I.I. money song for the third time in a row. This is Miles . . . Miles O'Barbwire, and I've gone plumb loco."

The jacked-up yellow truck that speeds by me in the opposite direction belongs to one Cole Clay Ellum. I'll remember the expression on his face for as long as I live. Terror. Sheer terror. It's a beautiful thing.

My voice continues to come out of the speakers. "Here's a little number called 'Jugular Clown Machine' that's sure to get your blood circulating this morning. You're listening to K.I. 'Yippee' I.I.—where LouseTrap is getting its start."

Winslow's wicked guitar threatens to blow holes in my speakers. I turn it up, anyway, and point my car toward Macy's.

We need to talk.

Extension Four

"Lifeline," I say. "We're here to help."

The line goes dead. We get that a lot. Girls think they're ready to talk, but when they hear a real voice, they lose their nerve. They always call back, though. With Caller ID, it's easy to check.

Okay, so maybe you're wondering why a pregnant teens help line would have Caller ID. It's not what you're thinking. Lou Ann had to order the service because of all the obscene phone calls we were getting, back before I started here. Calling an adoptive services agency to talk dirty; how *massive* a loser would you have to be? Of all places for a phone perv to call, why us? Maybe those guys liked the fact that they were sure to get a female on the other end. Maybe they were looking for "action." Lord knows I could've given them a big long phone list of good prospects. I'd never really do that, of course, but you ought to see some of the girls who come in here. From their clothes and makeup, I'm guessing they don't refuse many offers.

Sometimes I wonder if my mom—my biological mom—was one of these girls. Was she a fifteen-year-old in a Judas Priest T-shirt riding around on the back of her boyfriend's Harley? I wonder if she had tattoos and a quarter-inch layer of purple eye shadow. Did she get stoned a lot?

Probably.

But it's not like I hate her. She made at least one good decision in her life. When she got herself knocked up, she didn't run off and get an abortion. That's the reason I'm here. Not just in this chair, but alive . . . existing on the planet.

I'm lucky.

I look at my dad, my real dad, the man who raised me, and he's just what you look for in a father. Reads the sports page in the morning. Scares boys that come to pick me up. Makes dumb jokes and puts animal crackers in my suitcase whenever I leave town. He's a building contractor. He put up most of the homes in Rancho Del Lago Estates. My mom, my real mom, she's on the board of directors out at the club. She used to be a teacher before they adopted me and Hans. Now she teaches Sunday school. These are the genes I want to believe I have, and most of the time, I'm able to.

What would happen if I actually met my biological mother today? She'd probably be just like one of these girls who come in to Lifeline, except seventeen years older. Maybe she's a drug addict. Probably couldn't even tell me who my biological father is. That's how they are. I don't hold it against them, but I can't pretend to be blind.

The hours I put in here count toward my community service requirement, but I was volunteering way before my senior year, before the hours even counted. Most of my friends hate their ComServ assignment, but this is something I believe in.

The phone rings again. I look down at the buttons. "Extension four!"

I yell it loud enough for Lou Ann to hear back in her office.

"Got it," she shouts back. And then, like always, she closes her office door.

One of the first things Lou Ann explained to me when I started working here was that volunteers don't answer extension four.

"The girls who call up on that line have special needs regarding privacy," Lou Ann drawled—she's got the thickest East Texas accent of anyone I know. "They want to make sure they're dealing with someone in charge."

If I wanted, I could see who's on the line by checking the Caller ID, but I try not to notice. When I have looked—by accident—it's been names that I don't recognize. Girls named Washington or Johnson, Rodriguez or Vizquel. Occasionally some notorious poor white trash family name. But that doesn't matter to Lou Ann. She treats every girl like a princess. She is the sweetest lady I know. I hate to say it, but some-times she's so sweet, she gets on my nerves. She's had me and Caitlin—the other student volunteer—over to her house for homemade ice cream so many times that I'm about ice creamed out. Lou Ann doesn't have any kids, and sometimes I think she tries to spread all her excess love with "the girls," and with Caitlin and me.

I think it's Lou Ann's reputation that convinces a lot of girls from Lee to come to us first. Well, maybe that and the ad we run in the school newspaper.

Lifeline Adoptive Services—a reasonable alternative.

Back when I was a freshman, the only ads you'd see in the paper would be for Bonanza or Whataburger, maybe one telling you to buy the year-book. Now it's a real battleground. Planned Parenthood drew the line by placing an ad in the paper, making it a breeze for anybody to just go pick up a handful of condoms. Or, if one of the contracep-tives happened to break, the happy couple could run by and sign up for an abortion. Yep, Planned Parenthood made it a real shopper's paradise. That's what made me politically active. A bunch of us from Fellowship of Christian Athletes put together a peti-tion to have the ad yanked from the paper. Lou Ann's husband, Larry, was our sponsor back then. It was his idea, and working on the project was how I origi-nally met Lou Ann. Anyway, once we got over five hundred signatures, there was a big school board meeting where anyone could get up and talk for a minute. Tons of people did, and most of them—

including me—said the school paper was no place for that sort of ad. I still remember Lou Ann's turn.

"If our board members approve of an organization that distributes contraceptives to teens and then arranges their abortions," she said, "surely they won't have a problem with me opening a drive-through Beer Barn next to campus to complement my undertaking business."

But it didn't work. Somehow the Planned Parenthood lawyers scared our cowardly board members into letting the ad stay. Since that defeat, ads routinely compete for the futures (or as Lou Ann says, *souls*) of teenaged girls. We put our quarter-pager right next to the Planned Parenthood ad. But we're not the only other option. I think there's, like, five different agencies all claiming to know what's best. Most of us offer pregnancy testing and counseling. Caitlin and I don't do any of that, we just hand out literature, put up flyers at school, answer questions over the phone, let them know that they've made a good decision. I always tell the girls that I talk to about how I wouldn't be around today if it weren't for somebody making the same decision they're making. When it's time for real counseling, Lou Ann or Miranda Hearst, the youth minister at First Baptist, handles it.

It's cool I work with Caitlin. We've been friends forever. She's not adopted, but her heart is in the right place. She's not much of a worker either. She repaints her nails everytime we work down here. She lets me handle all the calls and the walk-ins. The only time she answers the phone is when I'm on the other line. Since it's unusual for us to get more than three or four calls a night, there's not much left for her to do except fill me in on the news about Todd, her boyfriend, who's off playing football at Texas Tech.

Caitlin hates it when someone from school comes in instead of calling. That happens sometimes since we're less than a mile from Lee. It doesn't bother me; it's not like my friends are the ones getting knocked up. The girls who walk in get a little embarrassed, but we hurry to get a Coke in their hands, make them comfortable on one of the couches, and hand them pamphlets showing happy families with their adopted babies. Sometimes I know the girls' names, but most of the time I don't. Different social circles. That's all.

That's why it's half surprising when Leslie Aitken walks through the door. She's white, fairly well-off, and the daughter of my minister. She's also in honor society and the editor of the *Rebel Yell*, our school paper. The reason it's only half surprising is because, in addition, her nickname is Easy A. Everybody in eighth grade heard about her and Tyke Milton. She was the first white girl to start doing it. The scary part is that we're sort of friends. It would probably be more accurate to say we share a lot of the same friends, but I've always thought that she's sort of snotty. A couple of weeks ago in English, Mrs. Paulson told us, "Everyone should take out their notebook and pen," and Leslie says, "You mean *his* notebook and pen." *That's* the kind of person she is.

Leslie sees me immediately. Then she sees Caitlin. Caitlin makes me want to laugh. She's got her nail polish brush stuck there in front of her half-polished toes and you could fit a tangerine in her mouth. I figure this one's up to me.

"Want a Coke?" I ask Leslie.

"And the ice is broken," she says. That's just how she talks. "Sure."

So I get her one. We've got two couches facing each other in the front lobby. I walk around the counter and sit on one of them. "Want to sit?"

I push the Coke can across the coffee table separating the couches.

"Why not?" she says. She pops it open, takes a huge gulp, then just sits there looking around at the posters on the walls. I can't really think of any small talk.

"So what's up?" I say.

"The rabbit done died."

"Oh," I say. Then there's this pause before I remember the script Lou Ann had us rewrite in our own words then memorize. "Well, in coming here to Lifeline you've made the best possible decision for you and your baby. We'll make sure you get the best . . . "

"Whoa there, Jill," says Leslie, "I haven't made any decision. I'm investigating the possibilities. So rein in the Clydesdales on your little sales pitch."

"All right," I say calmly. "You want to see some of the brochures?"

"Remember. Your ad says strictly confidential. If anyone finds out, you two will fry."

I glance over at Caitlin. By now I'd need a grapefruit.

Two weeks later everybody in school knows about Leslie Aitken.

But I didn't tell anyone. Okay, I told Tina and Claire. But they *swore* they wouldn't tell anyone, and when I asked them about it, they both *swore* they hadn't. So I don't know where it's coming from. Caitlin, I guess. She should know better. On second thought, Leslie just probably told too many people herself.

In Mr. Warren's class a few days ago, a couple of boys, Tommy Parks and Rid DeLord, were giving her a hard time, doing their dueling Elvises.

"C'mon there, pretty Mama. How's about you and me gettin' us a honeymoon suite at the Heartbreak Hotel."

"Don't listen to that polecat's lies. I'm the one that's gotta hunka burning love for ya, Mama."

They haven't stopped calling her Mama all week.

It's not so much that people around school are surprised by the news about Leslie. The real gossip has centered on who the father is. With Leslie, you just don't know. She's supposed to have done about half the football team, along with the black student council president, her assistant editor on the *Rebel Yell,* and two of the band guys at the same time. (And I'm not talking about one of the nearly cool little rock bands that guys in school have put together. I'm talking about a couple of geeks in Marching Dixie—the school band.) But that last rumor's so gross, I've always been inclined to give Leslie the benefit of the doubt on it. In the last week, you'd never heard so many guys talking about who they *hadn't* doinked. Every time people thought they had it pegged, the guy in question would issue some sort of denial.

"I kissed her once when I was drunk at a party, but nothing else happened."

I was actually within earshot when Adam Scott claimed that Leslie had wanted to, but that *he* had said no. He had no idea where people had gotten the idea that they had gone through with it.

Yeah, right.

Leslie hasn't come back to Lifeline, and as far as I know, she hasn't called either. I want to ask her what she's decided, but I know I'll be risking death by fingernails. She's made herself pretty scarce lately skipping classes, but I didn't dress out in P.E. today, just so I could beat her to class.

The social studies building shares a courtyard with the back entrance to the vocational wing. You see a lot of the pregnant girls milling around back here taking a break from their two-hour family skills class. They used to carry around sacks of flour that were supposed to take the place of having a baby, but when the pregnancy rate here climbed over ten percent, the school went ahead and invested in those computerized dolls that cry in the middle of the night or whenever they're supposed to be hungry. I'm sitting on one of the cement benches looking for Leslie. I've made up my mind that I'm going to get her to come back down to Lifeline. I'm just minding my own business when this heavyset black girl pushes one of the high-tech dolls in my face.

"You mind holding him for me?" she says. "I gotta pee."

The girl's name is Rhonda, and she's probably six months pregnant, but she was big before any of this happened. I only know her because she came into Lifeline once and looked at our brochures. It appears she's decided to keep her baby. Poor kid.

"Won't you get in trouble?" I say.

"Naw, I'll only get in trouble if they see me leaving him balanced up on one the sinks in there. Germs and shit crawling all over him."

She's shifting from foot to foot, still holding out the dark-skinned doll. I grab one of its arms.

"Not like that," she says, pulling the doll back. "Like this."

Rhonda holds the baby with both hands against her chest.

"All right. All right," I say. "Just hurry up."

She gives me a suspicious look, but her bladder forces her to trust me. She waddles off and leaves me standing in the courtyard holding on to the doll. I'm just hanging out feeling foolish for about thirty seconds when the bell rings and everyone comes flooding out of their classes. My first reaction is to hide the baby somewhere, but there's no tree nearby to stuff it in. There's a garbage can, but I reject that idea. A pack of JV baseball guys walk by, and I swing the doll around behind my back, but something feels wrong. It's too light. I bring my hand back in front of me. I'm holding on to one fat little baby arm. The rest of the doll is bawling before it hits the ground fifteen feet away.

"Yo, Jill. Didn't know you dated brothers," says one of the sophomore jocks.

I give him a drop-dead look, and his buddies start laughing. Meanwhile, the baby is smack-dab in the middle of the sidewalk, crying and getting kicked around like a soccer ball. The next sound I hear is Rhonda's shriek.

She lumbers past me and falls intentionally but awkwardly onto the sidewalk, corralling her doll and protecting it from further abuse. She's swearing up a storm and stroking the fake baby hair. As she struggles to her feet, I notice the scrapes on both her elbows. But Rhonda doesn't seem to mind; she's spotted me.

"Prepare to die, girl," she says, the one-armed bawling robot cradled next to her chest.

I take a step back. A few students are stopping to watch us. I'm looking for a clear sprinting path.

"I was doing you a favor," I say as I relocate behind the bench.

"Some favor. Now I'm gonna have to start all over. Do you know how long a month is when you're trying to raise a child?"

I respond as quietly as I can. "You're carrying a doll around. It's not really a baby. Can't you just take out the battery? Make it stop."

"Come here. I'll rip your arm off, and we'll see if you cry."

"All I'm saying . . . "

"I don't want to hear it. Give me back his arm."

I want to toss it to her, but I think better of it. Rhonda's started to calm down. She no longer looks like she's going to dive over the bench and remove my limbs. She's bouncing the doll and still stroking its hair. She's even saying, "Shhh. There, there now. *Shhhh.*"

I hand the arm back over the bench.

"I really am sorry."

"Not as sorry as Henry here."

She pops the arm back in its socket, but Henry continues his crying. It's starting to drive me crazy.

"Why won't it stop?"

"I'm going to have to have Mrs. Kupp reset him. They'll bring me up for charges of abuse."

"They'll what?"

"The baby is programmed. If it's been beaten up, or dropped, or kicked, or burned, or had one of its arms yanked out, it cries until Mrs. Kupp opens it up and resets the little computer inside. Then you have to face charges of neglect in front of a student hearing in our class. Then they sentence you to more time with the doll."

Rhonda holds the doll out in front of her, licks a thumb, and tries to wipe a smudge off of it.

"Did you know he's programmed to start crying three different times between midnight and six in the morning?"

"Just tell them it was my fault," I say. "I'll even go in and tell them."

"Don't matter. It's the same as leaving your baby with some stranger who batters him. It's still your problem. I never should have let you hold him."

As Rhonda's telling me this, I see Leslie walking down the sidewalk. She's by herself, none of the usual crowd of fans and would-be grope partners walking along beside her. Maybe she'll come out of this a bit more humble. She sees me staring, and gives me a wink.

Then again, maybe she won't.

I show up the next day with a stuffed Winnie the Pooh. It's small, but cute. I got it at Hallmark. After second period, I wait outside the vocational wing for Rhonda. You can't help but spot her. The combination of her size and reputation creates natural personal space as she steps out of the building.

I move in beside her on the sidewalk. She doesn't even look at me.

"Whatchoo want?" she says.

"I got this . . . for Henry. I just wanted to say I'm really sorry. I should have taken better care of him. I thought maybe, after Henry plays with him, it would be something for your baby."

Rhonda takes the stuffed animal from me and lodges it between Henry's arm and body.

"I ain't decided yet," says Rhonda.

"Decided on what?"

"Whether to keep that baby or not."

"What?"

Rhonda can tell what I'm thinking. She shakes her head like I'm stupid. "Whether to keep it or give it up for adoption."

"You haven't been back into Lifeline. I guess I just assumed you were going to keep it."

"Well, Henry's teaching me a thing or two about what it's like to be someone's mama."

I want to urge Rhonda to come back into Lifeline and talk to Lou Ann, but I see Angie and Trish walking toward me, and I don't want to have to play Twenty Questions about what I'm doing with this two-hundred-pound black girl, so I break away from her as my friends approach. Angie's wearing this sinister little smile on her face, and Trish won't look at me.

"You read the *Yell* today?" Angie asks.

"I didn't even know it was out yet."

"You should pick it up," Angie says in this real nasty voice. "Let me know if you see anything interesting."

She and Trish start to walk off.

"On second thought," she says, turning around. "just keep it to yourself. It'll be good practice."

It's fifth period before I get my hands on a complete issue of the newspaper. Nothing catches my attention right off: FFA Officers Elected, Spring Beach Cleanup Looking for Volunteers (the second paragraph mentions the sixteen hours of ComServ credit seniors can get for it,) One In

THREE GIRLS SUFFERS FROM AN EATING DISORDER. Thanks for the news flash. When I finally get to what I'm supposed to be looking for, there's no doubt about it. It's Leslie Aitken's personal column. It's always on the back page of each issue, and it's got her picture right next to it. The column's called *Oediter's Complex*. You can see in the picture how proud she is of herself.

THE JOKE'S ON YOU

I'm not pregnant.

Never have been. Everybody just thinks so. Everybody includes my father, which explains why those of you calling my house haven't been able to reach me. He threw me out. I'm now residing with my former sister-in-law, Elizabeth. Not that I expect the phone to be ringing off the hook.

For a long time, I've wanted to do a story for the *Yell* that would take a serious look at the choices available to a pregnant girl at Lee High School. I planned on interviewing girls who were already pregnant, girls who've had abortions, Sandy Kupp, the head of the family planning class here, plus all of the city organizations that advertise in the *Yell* encouraging girls to turn to them in times of crisis. But the more I thought about it, the more I realized:

I've read stories like that before.

I wanted to write something unlike anything a typical reporter would do. That's when I got the idea.

I got pregnant.

Let me tell you. It's easy to do. I just told two high school volunteers down at Lifeline Adoptive Services, made them promise not to tell anyone, and within forty-eight hours I had received my first call from a friend asking me, "Is it true?"

All I said in reponse is, "I can't believe this is happening to me."

Good gossip travels fast, and everyone believes it.

Uh-oh. I'd better talk to Caitlin again.

I know it's not essential to this story, but I'd like to take a moment to thank all of the gentlemen here in school who've cleared up any misinformation about the nature of our past relationships. I can't imagine how people got their original seedy ideas. But before I do get too carried away with sociological aspects of my experiment, I'd like to tell you what I learned as a pseudopregnant teenaged girl in Deerfield: Everyone else knows what's best for you.

There are currently six ads in the *Yell* aimed at girls "in trouble." Although all of them offer pregnancy testing as well as something called "pregnancy counseling," the counseling varies greatly from location to location. I should know, I talked to them all.

Then Leslie writes a little bit about each of the places she called, making them all sound awful except for Planned Parenthood.

Planned Parenthood was the only place that asked me what I thought was the best thing for myself. The woman there actually listened more than she talked. The way people have made them sound, I thought they would be waiting for me at the door with a giant syringe full of saline solution. I thought there was probably a Dumpster full of fetuses behind the building, but they were really the only group that didn't try to force their beliefs down my throat.

At Lifeline, however, the teenaged "volunteers" give you a rehearsed speech about how you've made the right decision—as if setting foot in the office means you already know what you're going to do. They load you down with literature, glossy color brochures with lots of pictures of happy middle-class couples playing with their new babies in the rooms straight out of *Better Homes & Gardens*. Their enthusiasm makes it seem like they're making a commission on every girl who decides to put her baby up for adoption. A reminder: don't believe everything their literature says; they definitely are *not* confidential.

Still, they're far from the worst. The worst is a place listed in the phone book as Abortion Assistance. I called and told the woman that I had made up my mind that I wanted to have an abortion. She asked me my name. I decided after my incident at Lifeline to use a fake name. I told her it was Esther Prim, and she didn't even laugh. She wanted to know how old I was, so I told her sixteen.

"Well, you know, Esther," the lady told me. "Abortions without parental consent are illegal for minors, but I think we can get you fixed up. We'd like to meet face-to-face."

"What for?" I asked.

"It's best if we can see for ourselves how old you look. Plus we can give you materials we have. *And*, we'd like to do a pregnancy test just to see how far along you are."

The creepy part was that she even offered to pick me up. I thought this group sure must be anxious to perform abortions. The lady came and picked me up outside my ex-sister-in-law's apartment complex and took me out to her pleasant country home. She scrambled to cue up a videotape while I admired her collection of antique dolls. She had me sit down. She dimmed the lights, then used a remote control to start the video.

I've sat through all four *Hellraiser*s, three *Friday the 13*s and I've even watched Jody Anderson at Bonanza's All-You-Can-Eat Chicken-Fried Steak Day, but nothing could have prepared me for the gruesomeness of that video.

It was a homemade fake documentary in which "doctors" with utensils that resembled miniature pruning saws ripped open screaming young girls and pulled out bloody, writhing hunks of flesh that were supposed to be fetuses. For the grand finale, the camera zoomed in on hideous remains tossed into a blood-caked bedpan. You could make out a tiny head with the lips sort of quivering, and they'd dubbed in the word "Mommy."

I think it was supposed to make me sick, but for some reason, all I could do was start laughing. That seemed to make the lady, who had been so nice up until this point, very angry.

"What do you think is so funny?" she asked as she stopped the tape. "Is this what you want to do to your baby?"

"The thing inside me isn't even the size of a penny. I hardly think it's speaking English yet."

"Do you think you'll still get into heaven if you kill your child?" she asked.

"Does this mean you're not going to help me get an abortion?" I asked.

"There'll be no abortion for you," she said. "The first thing we'll do is call up your parents, Esther."

She was starting to creep me out, so I played along with it.

"No, please, don't do that. It'd kill them. Maybe I should think about it some more."

My Oscar-caliber performance earned me a ride back into town. Since then, my sister-in-law has received phone messages every day warning her that her daughter is in grave danger and urging her to speak to me.

All in all, it's been a great laugh.

Everyone in school is talking about Leslie's story. Somehow it's turned her into the most popular girl in school. The same people who were calling her Easy A behind her back last week are having to dust off their eighties' slang dictionaries just to describe her marvelousness now.

"She's so *radical.*"

"She really takes it to the *edge.*"

Well, excuse me while I blow chunks.

And in the same time she's become Miss Instant Cool, I've been zeroed. I couldn't be less popular if I joined the debate team.

To everyone in school, I am the gossip, the person you can't trust. Never mind the countless promises that were made along the way. I told two friends; they promised not to tell anyone. They swore the people they told to the same code. But it's easily traced back to me. Why me and not Caitlin? Because I admitted I told a couple of people. She still swears she didn't, but I don't believe her. She's even had the nerve to treat me like everyone else has been treating me — like shit.

For the sixth day in a row, I'm eating by myself. I always let Hans take his sophomore buddies to lunch in the Saturn because I'm usually riding with Caitlin or Tina or Angie or Trish. But not anymore. They're hardly speaking to me, let alone splitting nachos at Taco Cabaña. Caitlin even quit her assignment at Lifeline. She was nearly done with her ComServ hours anyway. I hear she's going down to the Coastal Cleanup. Anything to show off that tan.

I haven't sunk so low that I'm paying for cafeteria food. I've got a Diet Pepsi and a bag of Fritos and I'm sitting underneath a tree in the cafeteria courtyard pretending this is what cool people do. I've gotten so used to the silent treatment that I brought along my Discman, and I'm grooving to Jars of Clay. It's a beautiful day, the sort of day where we would have decided to sit out on the patio at TCs. I close my eyes and imagine myself there. Just goofing.

Lying back with my eyes closed, I sense an eclipse. The sun has somehow been blotted from the sky. I shiver from what I try to convince myself couldn't be a chill. I open my eyes. The world has been blotted out by Rhonda Washington. I have to lean back to get her in reasonable focus. Henry, Winnie the Pooh tucked underneath his arm, completes the panorama.

"You busy?" she asks.

I think about it: I was reclining, eyes closed, listening to music, nearly sleeping. I can't think of a lie that would cover all those bases.

"Not really," I tell her.

"Can I talk to you some more about giving your baby up for adoption?"

I shouldn't have come to the party in the first place. I probably wouldn't have been invited, anyway, except that it's at Jimmy Hall's. He graduated last year, so he didn't know I was no longer cool. There are a lot of people who graduated last year here, which means I'm not completely ignored. I sip on a wine cooler for most of the night, and I try to look real interested in whatever people are saying to me so I don't look like a total martyr.

All my friends are here. They're the ones guarding the keg, laughing hysterically, and occasionally falling down. I hate it when they get like this. Well, sometimes it's fun, but I've always got to be the one to make sure everyone gets home safely.

Someone taps me on the shoulder. It's a boy. Probably a freshman up at Central from the looks of his Wildcat tank top and the fact that he's holding some weird kind of expensive bottled beer. When you live in a college town your whole life, you learn to recognize freshmen. He's sort of cute. He leans in to say something to me. I turn my ear toward his mouth.

"Can you keep a secret?" he says.

I start to nod, but the wild hyenas at the beer keg launch into a new fit of hysteria.

I get it.

I stay inside the house for the rest of the night. The freshman, Mike's his name, keeps following me around, trying to apologize. He tells me that my friends put him up to it. He says they told him I would think it was funny. I want to stay mad, but he's the only person I really have to talk to. Besides, he smells all right—not drunk—and he's wearing a crucifix on his necklace. He's asking me all kinds of questions about my family and where I want to go to school, which is strange because most of the time guys are more interested in telling you stuff about themselves. It must be an hour later that Caitlin and Trish and Angie come staggering through the house, standing up by hanging on each other's shoulders. Angie's twirling her key ring around her index finger.

"Are they gonna be all right?" Mike asks.

"Probably," I say.

But neither of us say anything for a few moments after the front door shuts behind my friends, the drunks.

"I think I'd better drive them home," I say.

"Yeah," says Mike. "Good idea."

I grab my purse and head for the door.

"Jill!"

I turn.

"What's your last name?"

"Stephenson."

"Thanks," he says. Then I'm out the door.

It's not difficult catching up with my former friends. Caitlin must have lost arm to shoulder contact at some point, because she's flat out in the lawn on her face. Angie and Trish are somewhere between crying and laughing.

"Why don't y'all let me drive," I say.

There's a pause in Angie's and Trish's laughing, but then they explode again and manage to ignore me.

"I'm serious. You could get hurt."

This time they stop.

"And you always know what's best, don't you?" Trish says. "Sure, why not?" She lobs the keys to her Camry high in the air. "I'll bet you can't wait to tell everyone about us at school Monday?"

"Who could I tell?" I say, catching the keys. "Everyone's here."

"Maybe that new friend of yours. What's her name?" Trish pretends to think for a minute. "Aunt Jemima?"

"You're such a hypocrite, Trish. You've told people's secrets before."

"Name one!" says Trish, getting suddenly angry.

"You and Leslie and Angie . . . skinny-dipping . . . Canyon Lake . . . with Clint DeFriesz and those guys. Tell me when it rings a bell."

She's so cold busted she doesn't know what to say. "*You—*"

"That's not even the point," Angie says, cutting off whatever name Trish intended for me.

"Well, what is the point?" I say.

"That you're judging everyone. All the time. When you told people Leslie was pregnant, you were, like, so appalled. Not worried or upset. You were just interested in making sure she was going to put the baby up for adoption."

"That's why no one tells you anything."

I look down on the ground where the voice came from. Caitlin's managed to roll over on her back. "It's because everyone knows how you'll freak out or quote the Bible or something. That's why I never told you."

Rob Thomas   78

"Told me what?"

Trish says, "Shut up, Caitlin. You're drunk."

"I don't wanna shut up." Caitlin tries to stand up, but settles for propping herself up with her hands behind her back. "Jill always knows what's best for everyone else. For so long I thought she really did. If I had listened to her in the first place, everything wouldn't have gotten so screwed up. That's why I volunteered down there."

"Caitlin, stop!" Trish says.

But now Caitlin's looking at me.

"But it's too hard. It's too hard being your friend and living up to everything you think is the right thing to do. What would you do? If you'd been Leslie. What would you have done?"

"You know what I would have—"

"You think you know," says Caitlin, "but you can't know unless you've been there. Could you have really had a baby, Jill? What would your parents have thought? I know you. Everyone staring at you. Eight months pregnant. Walking down the halls at school. You couldn't have dealt with that. It's so much easier being one of the ones staring, isn't it?"

"What are you saying?" I ask her.

"I'm saying I did the same thing you would have done."

"What did you do, Caitlin?" I ask. I'm starting to feel dizzy.

"Figure it out," she says.

The other girls have quit trying to stop Caitlin

from talking. They're all staring at anything but me. Caitlin doesn't know when to shut up. She never has.

"And it's not like I'm the only one."

And I know exactly who she's talking about. People can be so gullible.

Inside the house people begin shouting. The front door swings open, and a couple of football players come flopping out. They're swinging at each other, trying to rip each other apart. Predictably, a crowd follows them. Well, it wouldn't be a party without at least one fight. I turn back toward three of the most privileged girls in Deerfield.

"Here," I say, tossing the keys back toward Trish. "Drive safely."

They hand out the new issue of the *Rebel Yell* in civics. We've been given the final minutes of class to work on homework, but I'm not up to it. I scan the headlines: BLOOD DRIVE NETS SEVENTY PINTS, SOFTBALL TEAMS GEARS UP FOR POSTSEASON RUN, TWILLEY CHOSEN ACADEMIC DECATHLON COACH.

Boring. Leslie's column is about how she got to go backstage at Lollapalooza.

"The guys in Metallica are so down-to-earth," she gushes.

Then I see the ads. I don't know why we're still bothering to run one. Leslie's last column killed us. I think we may have gotten one call from Lee all month. I notice the ad for Abortion Services, and I remember something bothering me. Something about a doll collection.

After class I borrow a quarter and stand around until one of the pay phones becomes available. I unfold the *Yell* and dial the number in the ad. I can almost picture the phone ringing.

"Abortion Services," comes the voice. "Let us help you."

The drawl is unmistakable.

"Lou Ann," I say. "This is Jill. I quit."

"But it's Friday night!"

Mike is being whiny on the phone, but he's doing it in a funny way.

"I know."

"On Friday nights people go out. It's sort of like a tradition in our country. I think you might enjoy it."

"I told you. I'm baby-sitting for a friend."

"That's not a baby, Jill. That's a robot. On *Star Trek*, you can flip open a panel on Data's head and shut him off. Try that."

"I could have gone the rest of my life without discovering I'm dating a Trekkie."

"We prefer to be called Trekkers."

There's a moment of silence while I wonder whether Mike knows how cute he is. He probably does.

"Did I tell you she's going to keep it?"

"Keep the robot?"

"Keep her baby," I say. "She's out with Letty and Darla tonight celebrating. She said she's going to keep the baby up all night dancing. Get even with it for all the kicking."

"You think that's healthy? Isn't she due any day?"

"Three weeks," I say, "but I wouldn't worry about her. She is so careful. She carries around a thermometer and calls her doctor if she's a tenth of a degree high. She's eating a sackful of carrots a day, complaining the whole time. She always carries around enough cab fare that if she goes into labor, she can make it to the hospital from anywhere in Deerfield. She makes me quiz her on her Lamaze stuff."

"I guess instinct sort of kicks in," he says.

"Not for everybody," I say.

I remember sitting around Caitlin's parents' pool watching Live Aid when we were little kids. They showed the pictures of the starving people in Ethiopia, and we ran in and took the credit card out of her dad's wallet and donated ten dollars each. We thought we had done our part to change the world. My mother probably could have taught us something about sacrifice.

My real mom.

Blue Santa

I can't believe how good I feel. I shouldn't. I've hardly slept in two weeks. Viet and Ann kept saying I needed to go home and get some sleep, but how could I miss any of this? It keeps me on some kind of natural high.

Our Key Club—it's sort of a high school Kiwanis Club—has collected almost four hundred toys in the past sixteen days, and we're finally getting to do the fun part: deliver them. I've spent every afternoon this week down at the police station wrapping and sorting gifts: Tonkas go into the under-seven boys barrel, Hot Wheels to the eights and over. Dolls that don't do anything wind up in the pre-three girls stock. Dolls that spit up, wet, cry, mess their pants, blink, clap, talk, etc., get dropped in the four-to-six-year-old girls' barrel. Barbies—Malibu and otherwise—are for the seven and overs.

You wouldn't believe the stuff people have donated to us. Some people just come in and toss us their old-timey crap: wooden blocks, those antique vibrating electronic football games, Rock'Em Sock'Em Robots, Silly Putty, board games. But not everybody. Others actually go out and buy new stuff— Rollerblades, Mr. Microphones, Noodles. One woman actually brought in a Game Boy with three cartridges. I guess I had a pretty funny look on my face when she handed it to me.

"I told him that if he failed one single class, I was throwing it away," she said. "Well, at least this is better than doing that."

One of my duties as Key Club president is to make sure that every house gets an equal share of the cool stuff and the junk. The Game Boy I'm stashing away for someone special.

The Deerfield Police Department sponsors Blue Santa every Christmas, but we do most of the real work. They just gave some space and put together a list of families that'll get the toys. Some with fathers locked in jail. Some the victims of crime. All the families are poor. Ann, Viet, and I are riding with Officer Reggie Davis, who has his police radio turned down and his car stereo cranking out Christmas songs. Tonight's supposed to be a night off for him, but in between "What Child Is This?" and "Sleigh Ride," he tells us how he wouldn't have missed this for the world.

"I've seen some awful things happen to the people in these neighborhoods," he says. "I want to be there to see something nice happen."

Around town, four other patrol cars with two or three Key Clubbers each are doing the same thing we are. It's weird, I've lived my whole life in Deerfield, and I've never been on the street we're cruising down right now. I'm completely stoked. I want to ask Officer Davis to turn on the siren, but I don't. He pulls up in front of a house. Viet grabs the video camera. I start gathering up the presents that've spilled out of their sacks. While I'm doing that, I find two boxes wrapped in silvery paper that I know we didn't use. I hold one up to examine it.

"Those are for my kids," Officer Davis says. "Finished up my shopping this afternoon."

That helps explain *his* merriness.

Ann edges in beside me and pulls out one of the stockings that we've stuffed with donated goodies: one Life Savers Storybook, two bottles of bubbles, one Spiderman comic book, one Hamburglar action figure, and three Power Ranger coloring books. On each of the stockings we've glittered and glued:

Lee High Key Club & Blue Santa
Wish You a Merry Xmas.

We spent twenty minutes during a meeting arguing about whether Xmas was okay. Viet, my vice president, said that it sounded too commercial, and that, on top of that, it was sacrilegious to shorten Jesus's name.

"X Almighty, Viet," said Allen, who I think just

joined Key Club because he's always had a crush on Ann. "Unless we're giving size seventy-six socks, we don't have space for the whole thing,"

Ann thought we should just put a Santa or reindeer or something like that on the stockings, but I explained that it would be better for the video if there was something that said Key Club on it. We're going to enter the service project video scrapbook contest the state organization puts on.

The kids at the first house freak when they see the toys. They start playing right away while their mother complains to Officer Davis about some loud neighbors or something.

"Get a close-up of their little Christmas tree with no presents, then shoot them playing with the ones we brought," I tell Viet. "Quick, get the little girl hugging her doll. Oh, yeah, and a shot of the sock."

One of the little boys throws his new football across the room. The pass is intended for his older brother, but it grazes Viet's head and knocks over a lamp. The mother chases the little boy into a bedroom, and we get to hear the spanking in progress. Then the crying starts.

"Ready?" says Officer Davis.

"Let's boogie," says Ann.

The episode doesn't spoil the perfect mood of the patrol car. The local station is now playing "Here Comes Santa Claus," and we're all singing along, Officer Davis the loudest. I can't believe how worth it this is all going to end up being. I remember for a moment how I felt last year when we went to the state Key Club convention. We felt like we worked really hard doing a car wash for muscular dystrophy and a town square cleanup, but when the state president made the announcements for the top service projects in the state, we didn't even place. It was the first time in the last decade, according to our sponsor, Mr. Burke. Of course last year's president, Byron McElroy, wasn't much of a motivator or organizer. He didn't even call the *Deerfield Herald* when we did the city cleanup, and we could have done twice as many cars at the car wash if he hadn't insisted on vacuuming and Armor All-ing. Good guy, bad president.

The second house goes better than the first. The kids are cleaner and better behaved. They open their presents one at a time, which is something my sisters and I can't even manage. Of course, when you're only getting one thing for Christmas, I guess you'd want to make it last. The calmness of the kids makes it easier for Viet to get good shots of the presents they open. Viet has a friend who's an RTF student up at Central. He'll add some slow motion and sad music. That's the kind of thing that always wins the contest.

The next three apartments we hit are all in the same scary complex. It's not until we get to the third apartment that I see the first dad of the night. He's in one of those white tank-top undershirts, and he has a baby pressed to his shoulder. You can see where the baby's spit up all over him—a couple of times at least. Officer Davis told us the man's wife is a junkie who's in and out of jail and rehab. The apartment is pretty barren. There's a couch, a dining room table, three duct-tape-repaired chairs pushed in around it, and that's it. Dinner—beans and saltines—is still out on the table. Then I see something funny. The door has four locks: the handle, a dead bolt, a chain, and a sliding bar. What for? There's nothing in this place anyone would want to steal.

In addition to the baby, there's a three- or four-year-old girl and two boys. One looks seven or so. The other might be about nine.

Two boys—that's a problem, because they only listed one boy on the information sheet, so I only put one gift for one boy in the sack for this address—a Nerf ball rifle that shoots these little golf ball-sized sponges. I can't figure out what I should do. It's our last stop, otherwise I'd trade something out of one of the other sacks. Maybe the boys can just share the present. From the looks of the younger boy's clothes, they're pretty used to sharing already.

While I'm thinking about what I should do, Ann takes the baby from the father's arms and makes little baby sounds at her. The father seems to lose his pained expression for a moment as he smiles at our club secretary. In that moment, a plan comes to me. I walk nonchalantly over to Officer Davis.

"Hey, can we use your police radio?" I whisper.

"What for?" he says.

"We're one boy toy short. We can have one of the other cars bring us something."

"Wait here," Davis whispers. "See if you can stall."

The sound of the door shutting behind Davis makes everyone look over at me before I'm really ready to pull this off.

"What's up?" says Viet, not helping.

Failing to come up with anything better, I say, "Caroling."

I talk to the kids.

"Before we open gifts, we like to sing a Christmas song or two." I try to think of the longest one I can get through. "Do you know 'The Twelve Days of Christmas'?"

The boys nod, but appear both mystified and reluctant.

The little girl shouts "Yeah!"

"All right, then." I glance up at Viet and Ann who are agape. *On the first day of Christmas, my true love gave to me . . .*"

The boys chime in unenthusiastically "*. . . a partridge in a pear tree. . .*" The little girl doesn't really know the words, but she stumbles through loudly.

At least Viet is getting this on tape.

We're up to four calling birds when Officer Davis makes it back into the apartment. He's holding one of the silver boxes.

"All right," I say. "Good enough. Time for presents."

The boys look at each other suspiciously, but say nothing.

At all the other houses, *I've* distributed the gifts, but this time, Officer Davis plays Santa. He gives the little girl her gift first. She tears open a Miss Piggy tea set for six with bread-and-butter plates and soup tureen. She insists that we all have a cup of imaginary tea, which we fake sip. Ann slugs hers down and asks for another.

"These two are for the boys to share," Officer Davis says.

They open the Nerf ball rifle first, and I can't help thinking that this is a perfect gift. There's nothing they can break in this whole apartment. They'll have to play hunter and hunted, though, not war, since they just have the one weapon. The second gift is the one wrapped in the shiny silver paper. The boys go at it from both ends, and within seconds, the paper is shredded. The picture on the outside of the box is of a portable stereo, and I'm worried that the boys will think that's what it really is. On the other hand, that's probably just what I'd think. These kids look like they're used to low expectations. They're more careful about opening the box than they were about unwrapping it. The first thing I see is Styrofoam, then I realize—it really is a stereo.

At first the boys look too stunned to move. But within seconds it's plugged in, and Officer Davis has helped them tune in the Christmas station. The little girl comes up and hugs me, but she keeps holding on to my legs, and I realize she's trying to dance with me.

"Bobby said there was no such thing as Santa," she says.

But I don't know who Bobby is. One of her brothers, I guess.

"Ready?" I ask my group.

As we're heading down the stairs of the apartment building, we can hear the stereo being changed over to the all-hits station. A moment later it's back on Christmas songs. It may be the boys' gift, but tonight the father's running the show.

Back in the patrol car we're all pretty silent. Finally Ann speaks. "That's probably the best Christmas gift they've ever had."

If there wasn't a steel-mesh screen between her and Officer Davis, I think she'd hug him.

"It'll get pawned first thing when their mother gets back," says Officer Davis, looking sad for the first time all night. "I hope they get some enjoyment out of it now."

Our car is the last back to the station. I get reports back from all of the teams. We've got photos, video. Allen took a tape recorder and got testimonials from some of the kids who received gifts. A reporter from the *Herald* rode in one of the cars, and a yearbook photographer rode in another. We're a lock at May's convention. I can see it already . . .

"And for the outstanding service project performed this year in the state of Texas . . . Lee High School."

Thunderous applause.

I'm fantasizing about my acceptance speech during the ride home with Viet.

"What are you playing?"

I focus more intently on the Game Boy as the stream of tumbling blocks encroaches upon the top of the screen.

"Tetris," I say.

We pass under one of the strings of gold garland and Christmas lights that they hang across Main Street during the holidays.

"Sweet gift," he says.

Gift? I think to myself. *I earned it.*

Half a Mind

Yes, it's me.

Turn and look all you want. It's me sitting here with just who you think it is.

Don't try to look away and pretend you're not staring. I see you. You're wondering if he's really holding my hand? Well, he is. He loves me. I love him.

Get used to it.

Now if I can only get my heart to stop beating so fast. If I can just act natural. Thank God for french fries. They give me something to do. Use my free hand. Dip a fry in the ketchup. Watch it all the way up to my mouth. Chew.

Antonio's At The Falls. Everyone comes here. It's just a burger place, but it overlooks the river, and you can sit out on the deck watch river rafters, and listen to bug zappers frying mosquitoes. The waitress comes over and asks if we want refills on our drinks. I say yes, even though it'll be my third one.

Then I feel a foot under the table. It's his rubbing up and down against my leg, and I look across the table and he's smiling *that* smile. Nothing else matters anymore. I thank God again. This time for The Willows.

No one else wanted to work out there. That's why I picked it. That's just how I am. I do lots of stuff no one else wants to, and I like lots of stuff no one else likes. Sometimes that's good. Like when Mom buys Neapolitan ice cream. There used to be six of us before Debbie went off and got married, but none of the others wanted to eat the strawberry, so I got twice as much as anyone else. Smart, huh? And that's not all. I'm the only one I know who still likes Michael Bolton or Sweet Valley High books. I was reading one in class one day—I think it was *Seaside Rendezvous*—and this girl started laughing at me, saying it was a junior high book. I'm trying to show her that it's not. It's Sweet Valley *High*, after all, but she's already snatched it from me and is reading one of the kissing scenes out loud to the class. That's when Miss Price stops her and makes her give me back my book.

"Laura"—she said my name loud enough so that everyone was listening—"marches to her own drummer."

People shut up when she said that.

See, that's how I am. I march to my own drummer. Working at The Willows is just another example. The Willows is the place where they treat head injury patients, and even though everyone at Lee High is required to get in two hundred hours of community service, and even though Mr. Reynolds, the director of The Willows, came out to the school—personally—and made this big speech begging for volunteers, I'm the only one who signed up. That meant there was plenty for me to do out there every Saturday from eight to five, but I didn't mind. I'm a hard worker.

There was another reason I didn't mind.

Jason Leary.

I didn't know he was going to be there, so don't get the idea that's why I picked The Willows. If I *had* known, I probably would've signed up for something else. It's just too embarrassing. I mean I feel like I probably blush whenever I hear his name.

Jason Leary.

He graduated two years ago. I didn't have him in any classes or anything. I was just a sophomore then. Besides, he was dating Tiffany Delvoe, and she was voted most likely to have her own swimsuit calendar. I had the worst crush anyway. I used to sit on the benches by the parking lot before school and pretend to be reading, but really I was watching Jason. He'd pull up on his motorcycle. I don't know what kind it was, but it was purple. By the time he'd get the kick-stand down, a crowd—*the* crowd—would be gathered around him spoiling the view. Sometimes they'd shift, though, and I'd get a good look at him. Jason kept his hair long. Shoulder length. That's what got him kicked off the football team. (Well, some people say it was because of drugs, but those people are just jealous.) Anyway, his hair was brown, but it had natural highlights. I know they were natural because Debbie tried to highlight my hair once, so I know what it looks like when they're fake. But his teeth! In one of my SVH books it described Cody, the new boy in school, as having teeth so white that Cindy, the preacher's daughter, imagined them as the picket fence that would some day surround their cottage. That's how white Jason's teeth were to me.

He looks different now, but not much.

I heard the news last year in algebra. Two boys in front of me were whispering back and forth, but I could hear what they were saying clear as a bell. People never seem to whisper very quietly around me. There's no one I trust enough to whisper things to, but I know if there ever was, I'd whisper a lot more softly than everyone else does.

Anyway, they were saying it served him right.

. . . for showing off . . . for riding without a helmet . . . for drinking . . .

I had to ask to leave class when I figured out they were talking about Jason. I started crying in the girls' bathroom. I don't know why. I mean, I'd never talked to him or anything. He was just this beautiful boy. It was like I was Jennifer from *Spring Break Affair* and he was Troy, the ski lift operator.

They were in love. They had always been in love. "Someday," the mountain seemed to promise, "these two will meet."

He's still beautiful. Just different looking. His hair

is cut short. His parents make him keep it that way, but I don't think Jason cares one way or the other. One thing about his haircut, though: With it this short, you can see the little pink scars that crisscross at the top of his head. He doesn't wear an earring anymore either. There's something a little funny about his eyes now, too. It's like they're not lined up quite right. His left eye's just a bit higher now than his right. But you really have to be looking to figure that out. His teeth? The same picket fence.

Because I was the only one who volunteered for The Willows, they were real nice to me out there. They let me do a little bit of everything. Make coffee. Clean the bathrooms. I put up the chairs in the cafeteria and wiped the walls when the patients were done eating. I helped Buddy, the giant male nurse, get the patients when it was time for physical therapy. They would send Buddy for the ones that needed someone to lean on. I'm not really that small myself, so Buddy would walk on one side of a patient and I walked on the other. With some of the patients we were just there for support. Some had to wrap their arms around us. That's what Jason would do. Or he used to, when I first got here. The first time Jason put his arm around me, I nearly fainted. Now he walks by himself, but he still kind of reminds me of my dad trying to make it to his bedroom after a long night down at the Black Cat Lounge.

The first time Jason ever talked to me was when I was helping Buddy take him to physical therapy.

First he spoke to Buddy. "You're black," he said.

And then Buddy said, "Congratulations. Guess they'll be discharging you any day now." But Buddy was joking.

Jason didn't care. His head swiveled around. He stared at me and then showed me *that* smile.

"Big titties," he said.

Then he reached out to touch me . . . touch them, but Buddy smacked him on the back of his head.

"Tell her you're sorry."

"Sorry," Jason said. He got this real sad look on his face and reached out for a hug. I was afraid he was going to start crying, but when I hugged him he wrapped his arms all the way around me, and he touched them. It happened so fast, though, I couldn't swear to it.

After we dropped Jason off at physical therapy, Buddy told me not to take anything Jason said personally.

"There's still a screw or two up there that needs tightening," he said. But that ended up being one of things I liked about Jason—his honesty. He'd just tell anyone whatever he's thinking. I've never been able to do that. That's why people just walk all over me.

After a while, they—Dr. Conathan and Dr. Ruiz—let me hang out in the rec room when I'd come in, and that didn't feel like work at all. I played a lot of checkers, a lot of Chinese checkers. I couldn't get anyone to teach me how to play backgammon. My favorite thing, of course, was getting to read to them. After a while, I had my own little group: Jason, Brittany, Mr. Hundley, and Mrs. Speck. Mrs. Speck was deaf, but she liked sitting in a circle with us.

I read them *Lifeguard Summer* first and everyone seemed to enjoy it. I was going to follow it up with *One Boy Too Many*, but Dr. Ruiz said I should "share less gender-specific material"—whatever that meant. Jason was right there when she said it. He broke in and right out loud told her, "You suck," but Dr. Ruiz ignored him. Later she handed me this book about rabbits. You've probably never heard of it. It's called *Watership Down*. I started reading that to them. At first I thought they'd hate it. I guess I thought I'd hate it, too, but I've ended up walking around school wondering what was going to happen to Fiver and Hazel and the rest of the rabbits. I really wanted to read ahead, but I forced myself not to. Now it looks like I should have.

I finished up all the hours they require for the community service credit in December, but instead of quitting, I started doubling up, heading out to The Willows on Wednesdays after school, not just on Saturdays. I told Dr. Ruiz I was doing it because I was never going to finish *Watership Down* by just going out there once a week. Which was true. But the bigger reason was that I thought Jason might have a crush on me.

Now even though I've read all about crushes, and I've had a million of my own, I'd never had the feeling before that someone had one on me. First off, he called me "Girl." I know that doesn't sound like much, and it's nowhere near as romantic as *Flesh and Blood Pen Pal* where Jake always calls Sarah, "Salvation," but you have to keep in mind what he was calling everyone else. He called Buddy "Giant," because he was I guess; Mrs. Speck "What," because it's all that she always said; Brittany "Sugar" since she had Sugar Pops for breakfast every day. He called Dr. Ruiz "Quincy" after some doctor on reruns.

Dr. Ruiz tried explaining it to me once. She said that, since his accident, there's neurological something-or-other that's missing a synapse or something- I didn't really understand, but she told me to think of a traffic jam in Jason's brain, but I didn't really like thinking about that. I think the truth was that Jason just liked calling people by nicknames. He had them all fooled, but not me. There are a lot of people with breasts at The Willows, but I was the only one he thought of as "Girl."

The second thing that made me think that Jason liked me happened when his parents were visiting. They offered to take him into Baskin-Robbins for some ice cream, and he said, "Can Girl come?" If I wasn't already sure I was in love with Jason by then, there was no doubt in my mind after the trip. Heading into town in his parents' car, Jason stared out the window in the same thrilled way that everyone else watches a movie. The Willows is a few miles out in the country, and the farm-to-market road curves through the Hill Country. Jason pointed out some cows trying to make a baby and said, "Check out the horses."

"Those are cows," his mom said, but Jason wasn't paying attention to her.

She leaned across the car and whispered to her husband. Naturally, it was loud enough for me to hear.

"He called the cows horses, Lyndon." She seemed so upset. And Mr. Leary shook his head like this was the worst news in the world.

"So what!"

For a second I couldn't even believe I was speaking out loud. It didn't sound like me. I think Jason was starting to rub off.

"What did you say?" Jason's mom growled at me, but she knew exactly what I said.

"You know what he's talking about. *Everyone* knows what he's talking about. Why does it matter that he gets words mixed up. Why can't you just be happy he's alive?"

Mrs. Leary turned to Mr. Leary and talked like I wasn't even in the car. "Remind me to have a little chat with Dr. Ruiz when we get back to The Willows."

"Shut up, Mom," said Jason.

She looked back at Jason, and suddenly I felt bad. I could tell she was trying not to cry.

At the Baskin-Robbins, I got a scoop of peanut butter ice cream. It was the only flavor that hadn't been touched. That's just how I am. I march to a different drummer. And you know what Jason did? He ordered peanut butter too.

"But you don't like peanut butter," his mom told him.

But the way he was shoveling it into his mouth, you sure couldn't tell.

When we got back to The Willows, Mr. and Mrs. Leary asked me to get Dr. Ruiz. Mrs. Leary sat in the lobby next to Jason, running her fingers through his hair while he spooned out the last bit of his ice cream. Dr. Ruiz rolled her eyes when I told her the Learys wanted to talk to her, but she followed me back to the lobby anyway. Jason was gone. Mr. Leary spoke up right when he saw Dr. Ruiz.

"We want to know when our son is going to get better."

Dr. Ruiz took a deep breath.

"We're pretty happy with your son's progress so far," she said.

"It's been a year," Mrs. Leary pointed out, her mascara all smudged.

I expected someone to dismiss me, tell me to leave the room, but it was like I was invisible. I heard Dr. Ruiz answering her with something like, "I don't think I need to remind you of the massive . . . " but by then I was halfway down the hall.

I was passing a janitor's closet on my way to the rec room when a hand shot out, grabbed my arm, and pulled me in to the darkened, bleach-smelling room.

I heard the word "Girl."

Then Jason kissed me.

My only other kiss also came in a closet. It was sixth grade, and Rainy Johnson had invited everyone in Mrs. Whitten's class over for a pool party. By the time it got dark, there were only six or seven of us left. Dad was supposed to pick me up, but of course he forgot. Anyway, somehow we ended up playing spin the bottle. The bottle landed on me twice, but the first time, Eduardo Cortez quit playing and told everyone it was a stupid game. The second time, Steve Wacker got up and actually beat me into the closet.

"Turn off the light," he said.

I did. Then his nose jabbed me in the lip as he kissed me on the chin.

"Shit," he said, "sorry."

I guess he got on his tiptoes, because next, I got a kiss on the lips. I was going to kiss back, but it was over before I knew it. After that I thought I might have a crush on Steve, but I heard that he was telling everyone that he felt me up in there, so I got over it. Like I always do.

Jason didn't miss when he kissed me. His lips landed in just the right spots. And I kissed back. Brother, did I kiss back. When Jason's hands came up the front of my body and started squeezing, I just let them.

"Girl," he said between kisses.

"Could you call me Laura?" I asked.

"Laura," he said.

He has them all fooled.

After that, the same thing started happening every time I went out to The Willows. At first I was worried, because in *Her Dark Secret*, Eric only wanted Patrice because of the dirty stuff. He *really* liked Shelly, who wouldn't give him the time of day. But Jason started calling me at home, and we'd talk all night sometimes, the nights Buddy was on duty. Eric *never* called Patrice to talk all night. He only called to say he was coming over.

During our phone calls, I did most of the talking, I guess, but Jason would sometimes tell me about how he wanted to be a veterinarian or a pilot.

"How about a veterinarian in Alaska," I said. "You could get your own plane—the kind with skis instead of wheels—and fly all over. Maybe even fix up seals or penguins when there are oil slicks."

"No penguins in Alaska, Laura," Jason said, but he didn't make me feel stupid like other people try to do when I say something wrong. "And no one would pay me to fix seals.

"Are you in slippers?"

He wanted to know if I was in bed. Everyone else wants him to learn to use the right words. I think Jason liked me because I took the time to learn his language. It became special to us, a secret code that just the two of us shared.

"Yeah," I said. I couldn't keep from smiling.

"Snug as a slug in a rug," said Jason.

When I'd come out to work, we'd walk around The Willows' grounds. They had him landscaping during the day when I was at school. He'd point out all the things he'd added: a walkway of flat stones surrounded by tree bark leading to the creek that ran along the north edge of the grounds; a two-leveled garden he'd made out of railroad ties; a concrete bird-bath with a working fountain.

For a month or so, everything was perfect. Then we got caught in the closet.

I think if it had just been Buddy, we'd have been left alone, but when he opened the door and saw us, he shouted, "Jesus Christ!" and Dr. Ruiz was walking by at the time.

She told me she wanted to see me in her office.

That's when she gave me the lecture. Before she even started, she got X rays out of her filing cabinet and stuck them up on that lighted screen.

"I think it's time you heard everything Jason's been through since the accident," she began. She said it in a voice that you could tell was supposed to be nice, but with some people that sort of voice doesn't fit. It doesn't fit with Dr. Ruiz.

"As you can see here," she said, pointing to a spot on the screen, "Jason's skull was badly crushed in the frontal . . . "

But I wasn't listening. I was nodding, but I wasn't hearing a word. I already knew the message, "Stay away from Jason." But she couldn't make me do that. Well, I guess maybe she could. But I was sure I could outsmart her. Something in the tone of her voice let me know she was summing everything up.

" . . . so you see how vulnerable that makes him, don't you?"

I nodded.

"I know he's a cute boy, and in many ways seems perfectly normal."

I nodded again.

"Do we have an understanding?"

"Yes, ma'am."

Then she let me go.

Jason got the same speech from Dr. Conathan. After that, we were more careful.

I got reassigned to the front desk. So except for when I was reading to the group, it was tougher to see Jason. Sometimes his parents would come to pick him up and take him out to dinner or to get ice cream. Jason loved getting off the grounds. Can you blame him? His parents, though, never seemed to remember me or really look at me. They'd come in and sign the guest book, and I'd call back for someone to get Jason, and they'd just sit there.

"Where to tonight?" I asked one time.

They looked at each other, and I figured they hadn't decided, because neither answered at first. Then Mr. Leary said, "The movies."

"Which one?" I asked.

"We're not sure yet."

"He wants to see the new Steven Seagal movie. I told him all about it. He's been dying to go."

But they acted like they didn't hear me. Buddy and Dr. Ruiz came through the door with Jason. Dr.

Ruiz started giving a progress report to the Learys. The phone rang. I answered it and pushed the buttons that forwarded the call to Dr. Conathan. Looking up, I didn't see Jason for a minute. Then I spotted him through the window. He was out in the parking lot getting on some visitor's motorcycle. I was out from behind the counter and through the front door in a split second. My heart felt like it wanted to leap out of my mouth as I got close and I saw that the keys had been left in the ignition. As I got closer to Jason I could see him staring down at the controls, but he wasn't doing anything and his shoulders were shaking.

"Jason, don't!" I shouted a couple of steps before I reached him. I tried to throw my arms around him, but he pushed me away. I fell backward onto my butt. He didn't really push me that hard. I can just be real clumsy sometimes.

"I can't do it," he cried. "I don't know how."

Buddy had caught up to me by then. The Learys and Dr. Ruiz were just a few steps behind him. The first thing Buddy did was pull the keys out of the ignition.

"Tell her you're sorry," he told Jason.

Jason wiped his eyes and looked down at me.

"I'm sorry, Laura. I screwed off."

"He called you Laura," Dr. Ruiz said, like it was some kind of surprise.

After the Learys left with Jason, I sat staring at the guest book. With nothing better to do, I started going back through the pages, seeing who all had come out to see Jason. The book only went back three months, but the only people I saw who came out were Jason's parents and a couple of other people with the same last name. The older guest books were under the counter. I flipped open the one from spring of last year, which was when Jason had checked in originally. It was like everyone from Lee High School had come out here then. Every day had five or six entries. Next to one of the names in the guest book is a Post-it note stuck on. It's Dr. Ruiz's handwriting saying, "Second visitor to claim she was groped by J. L."

Visiting Jason must not have been the thing to do for long. In last summer's book he was lucky to get a few visitors a week. Last fall he'd get one or two a month. By the time I started working here, he was left with relatives.

Dr. Ruiz called me at home later that night and fired me. She didn't really say *fired*. I was a volunteer, after all. But Dr. Ruiz told me they no longer needed me out there. That was bull. They need another three of me. I asked her if I could stay one more week, that I was nearly done with *Watership Down*. She asked me which page I was on and promised to finish it for me. I still don't know what happened to the rabbits. Jason called me at home when he got the news.

"They made them do it," he said. When Jason says "they," he's talking about his parents.

"Why?"

"I told them I loved you," he said.

He hadn't even told *me*. My whole life I'd been

waiting until I could describe myself as melting. Well, that's exactly what I did right then. It meant I could say something I'd always dreamed of. I tried to make it sound perfect. Grown up. Sexy—like on *Party of Five*.

"I love you," I said.

"Let's get married."

My life was better than a Sweet Valley High book.

In my head I started crossing off all the problems I could think of: I turned eighteen in January, so my parents couldn't stop me. Besides, Debbie got married because she was pregnant. I would be getting married for love. I was going to graduate in a month. I could get a job. Maybe something at the library, since I love books so much. Jason could do landscaping until he was able to go to college. We'd start off with a really small apartment. It would be a real hellhole when we rented it, but we'd work hard and somehow make it a home. By the time we were making enough money to buy a house, we'd almost hate leaving it, but we'd need to. We'd need the space for the children.

"Okay," I said.

When I gave him my answer, Jason laughed. Sometimes he does that when there's nothing funny. During some of the saddest parts of *Watership Down*, he would just bust out, and I mean loud, but the group started expecting that.

This time when Jason started laughing, I laughed too.

That brings me back to tonight.

We snuck Jason out of The Willows so we could celebrate. Well, that makes the escape sound like it was something out of *Mission Impossible*. It wasn't. He just walked down to the stream where he gets the flat stones, and I drove by and picked him up. He's allowed to leave the grounds; it's not against the rules, but you're supposed to check out, and we skipped that step.

It was Jason's idea to go to Antonio's At The Falls. I've never been in here. Dad came in here once, and when he got billed six dollars for a hamburger, he refused to pay, then created such a scene that they just let him walk out. A lot of tourists eat here in the summer. Some of the kids who live up on Society Hill actually eat here for off-campus lunch. When we first got here I didn't recognize anyone, but in the last half hour a whole group of Lee snobs have gotten tables.

And I can see them staring.

But that's all right. They can stare all they want.

That's my leg he's rubbing under the table.

The check arrives, and I count out sixteen of my baby-sitting dollars. As much work as Jason does around The Willows, they ought to pay him, but they don't, of course. It'll be different when we're married. Jason's so sweet. When I asked him who he wanted at the wedding, he said, "Just Laura." We're talking about having it in September. I heard the doctors talking about "Jason's timetable," and I remember them saying something about how, by the fall, they'll have done everything they can do.

Timm Trimble, this guy from school, comes walking up to the table and asks Jason, "How's it hanging?"

Timm doesn't even look at me. We were in the same homeroom for four years, but I get the feeling he doesn't know my name.

"I'll be back in a minute," I tell Jason. He tries to keep ahold of my hand, but I pull it away. Sometimes you have to do that with him. As I'm walking away from the table, I hear Jason asking Timm, "Who are you?" and that makes me smile.

I'm in one of the stalls in the women's rest room when I hear two girls walk in. I can see them through the crack in the door. One is Tiffany Delvoe, that girl in my grade that Jason used to date. I don't know who the second one is. It's the other one who I hear talking first.

"But she's a cow. A total cow. Do you think they're keeping Jason that doped up?"

"There's not that much dope in the world," says Tiffany.

"Yeah, well, he still looks pretty good. You can hardly tell."

"Eggs are scrambled, though." Tiffany says. Through the crack, I'm watching her put on lipstick in the mirror. "One day he's trying to get into A&M. The next day he's trying to tie his shoelaces. They say he lost half his mind."

Part of me wants to scream. I want to march right out and tell them that he can do his own shoes now. But I don't. I sit there and listen. The girl I don't know is at it again.

"They should make Jason one of those people on a commercial. You know, 'Wear a motorcycle helmet or this could happen to you.'"

Tiffany takes over.

"And then the camera could pan over, and you'd see that he has his arm around Laura Tuttle."

Both of them laugh their heads off.

It reminds me of that scene in *Best Served Cold* where Jessie overhears these girls talking bad about her, so she loses a bunch of weight and gets a new haircut and colored contact lenses and comes back after the summer and steals both their boyfriends.

But that's just a book.

I don't need to get even. I've got Jason Leary. And I don't care what he was like before. I don't need to. I love who he is now. And he loves me.

Get used to it.

The Laser

"Dr. Salazar will see you now," says my father's secretary.

I stand and try to work some of the crease back into my khakis. I'm making sure my shirt is tucked in when Dad shouts through the open door.

"*Now!* Dwight."

"Yes, sir."

I enter the large office and remain standing while he searches through the drawers of his desk.

"It's in here somewhere," he says as he sifts through a drawer.

"I've seen it before," I say.

"And you'll see it again." He glances up at me. "You need a haircut."

"Yes, sir."

"Aha! Here it is."

He slaps the brochure down on his huge oak desk.

"Take a look."

I fold it out and keep my eyes pointed toward the glossy photos, but I don't really see them. I know the images already. One of the photos is of a dormitory room. Twenty-four cots are lined up in six parallel rows. The next is of a guy in a crew cut climbing a rope, pulling himself over a barricade. The final one on the page is of a cadet, brows furrowed, gazing at a textbook.

And, of course, there's the headline.

HILL COUNTRY MILITARY ACADEMY AND PREP SCHOOL
MOLDING OFFICERS AND GENTLEMEN

Just what I need. Molding.

"I hope you don't think this is some sort of idle threat. You will get into a top school: Ivy League, Northwestern, Stanford. If you don't have the scores coming out of high school, it's off to Hill Country."

"I know all this," I say.

"Then maybe you can explain the seventy-eight on your English test. I had a nice long chat with Mrs. Paulson this morning."

He announces this as if it's going to be a big surprise, but he has nice long chats with all my teachers every week. I'm sure if he weren't their boss, some of them would tell him where he could stick his weekly chats.

"It was the fourth best score in the class. Did she tell you that? Besides, it was the same day as my trig test."

"Making excuses . . . like you grew up in the barrio." My father takes the brochure, holds it an arm length away—he's farsighted—and scans it down through his glasses as if he's already calculating the costs. "Besides, no one at Dartmouth checks to see what everyone else made. That round shape on the transcript looks like any other C to them."

"It's not on my transcript. It's just one test."

"I'm getting awfully tired of this lip."

"Yes, sir."

"Your next test is in a month?"

He knows the answer already.

"Well?"

"Yes, sir."

"Then I guess we know what you'll be doing with your weekends."

"Yes, sir."

"Other than getting a haircut."

English is my worst subject. I usually make A's, but I make A's in everything. English is just a tougher A. I don't think it's really me, though. I think it's English teachers. They assume that because they teach English, they can just invent answers. In math, if the answer is 256, that's the answer. You never hear a math teacher saying, "Two hundred fifty-six was intended as irony." Or, "What is the underlying meaning of the equation two to the eighth power?"

I like it when the answer is the answer. All the fuzzy stuff just makes me mad.

How can the ghost of his father compel Hamlet to such desperate measures?

I don't know. It doesn't say. The teachers don't *know* either. They just *think* they know the answer, and they're so sure about it that they figure they can mark my answers wrong and get me sent off to prep school. On this last test, Mrs. Paulson asked us her standard question after we finish a book: *Did you like* Hamlet? *Please explain why or why not.*

Here's what I would have liked to have written.

No.

I just don't.

I *never* know why. There are people who love reading books. Grampa, for example—he's always reading something. And there are people who can stare at a painting for hours. I went to Paris with my Dad two summers ago, and it took me an hour to see everything I wanted in the Louvre. Music? Same thing. I'm not saying there aren't some songs that I like, but when I do, I just like them. I don't sit around analyzing them to death.

But the question was worth *ten* points, so I put down that I liked it, even though I didn't, because I figured that's what she wanted to hear.

I liked Hamlet *because it was written by William Shakespeare (1564-1616), considered by many to be the greatest English dramatist and poet. Shakespeare, born in Stratford-upon-Avon, is best known for his great tragedies, including* Julius Caesar, Romeo and Juliet, Othello, *and* Macbeth. *Most of his plays were performed in London at the Globe Theatre.*

She gave me two points.

That's why I hate English, which is where I am when the office aide comes looking for me. Thank God or Dad, whoever's responsible for saving me from this B.S. we're doing now. We're actually putting Hamlet on trial for murder. I'm supposed to be Rosencrantz, who's going to be a witness for the prosecution. It's really dumb. Who knows what we're supposed to learn from this.

I'm sitting in the front row as I do in every class — Dad's orders — so when the aide asks for me, I can hear him clearly.

"They want The Laser in the library."

"Dwight," says Mrs. Paulson, "take your books. It looks like you won't be back before the end of the period."

I'm sort of suspicious about why they need me in the library, but I'm more than happy to collect my stuff and get out of English before testifying.

"Nice buzz, Laze," says the aide, pointing to my new haircut.

I don't know his name, so I don't bother responding.

As I walk across campus, I try to guess what they'll need me for. When your father is superintendent, you never know. Probably some teacher spent the weekend making a display of Indian migrations across Texas or made some new improvement to the

Lee High School Web page. They'll tell me some fake reason that they sent for me ("We want all the NHS officers to get a chance to see this first!"), when all they really want is for me to go home and tell Dad about it. It's fine with me. It gives me something to talk about during the after-school interrogations.

Mrs. Carlson, the librarian, calls me over when I enter. That's when I figure it out. It's my community service project. I'm reading for the blind. The good thing about the project—actually there are a bunch of good things about it—is that you don't have to read to them in person. You just read into this machine, some fancy sort of tape recorder. You can do it completely by yourself. Mrs. Carlson coordinates it. She gives you a long list of books you can choose from. She tried to pressure me into reading the ones *she* wanted, though.

"We're getting tons of requests for *Waiting to Exhale* and *The Bridges of Madison County*. You think you might like to do one of those?"

But what I was really interested in was knocking out two birds with one ComServ stone. I told her I wanted to do *The Catcher in the Rye,* which I had to read for Mrs. Paulson's class anyway. Besides—it's only 211 pages. It's what Dad would call a "shrewd move." He likes it when he sees me making "shrewd moves."

I've been waiting for the machine to be available again; I have to do three books before the end of the year.

"*Of Mice and Men.*"

"What?" says Mrs. Carlson.

"Can I do *Of Mice and Men*?"

I've been thinking about this for a while now.

1. It's required.

2. It's also short.

3. Someone's always got the video checked out at Blockbuster.

"Actually, Dwight, I'm afraid I've got some bad news."

"If it's already been done, I'll take *The Crucible*."

"It's not that," says Mrs. Carlson. She's obviously uncomfortable. It's something I'm used to around faculty members.

"What is it?"

"I got a call from the librarian up at Central, the one who's in charge of the reading for the blind program."

"Uh-huh."

Mrs. Carlson looks down at the countertop.

"They asked that we not use you anymore."

"Why?" I say, not really comprehending. It just doesn't make sense. I've always tested out as a top reader. I looked up any words that I didn't recognize in *The Catcher in the Rye* and made sure I got the pronunciation right. I kept my mouth three inches from the microphone just as they instructed.

"Don't worry about it, Dwight. They're just very picky up there. You know how snotty they can be at colleges."

"Did they give you a reason?"

"Dwight, it's not important."

"What did they say?"

Mrs. Carlson looks like she wants to crawl under the counter. She looks at me again, and decides that I'm probably not leaving until I find out.

"They said you didn't have any feeling."

"No feeling?"

"Well . . . no inflection."

I just stare at her.

"I wouldn't worry about it, Dwight. We've got something else in mind for you to pick up those ComServ hours."

"Like what?"

"Tutoring. We need someone with strong reading skills and some Spanish."

"Not interested," I tell her. I leave out how I think it's racist to assume someone knows Spanish based on skin color.

"How long did it take you to read *The Catcher in the Rye* out loud?" Mrs. Carlson asks.

"I got sixty-six hours and forty minutes' credit."

"But how long did it take? Really?"

I look at her suspiciously, but decide she's trying to help.

"A little over twenty hours. That includes setup time, and they said to read it to myself first. Plus, the instructions said to read slow."

"All right. Well, I can offer you a deal. I'll give you credit for your two other novels for three Sundays of tutoring—six hours each day."

I do the math in my head.

"Where do I sign?"

❖ ❖ ❖

I'd seen him before, but out of context it took me a couple minutes to figure out where. It wasn't until I heard him start humming some old Mexican jukebox standard that I was able to place him. The old man waiting on the library steps was Weedy Gonzalez, this groundskeeper who always had a song on his lips, a big grin on his face, and a gas-powered Poulan fish-line trimmer in his hands.

His name, I learn right off, is neither Weedy nor Gonzalez.

"Eli," he says, holding out his hand. "Eli Escobar."

One of the reasons it's tough to recognize him is because he isn't wearing the only thing I'd ever seen him in: the Deerfield ISD jumpsuit. His hair is slicked back and combed so that you can count where every tooth had sliced through the oily mess. He's wearing a short-sleeved dress shirt and a tie that doesn't match. At first I have the big-headed idea that he has dressed up for his tutorial. Then I remember—*everyone* east of the highway makes it to Mass on Sunday.

"Uh, yeah, I'm Dwight," I say as he waggles my hand up and down like he's trying to shake the watch off my wrist.

"Dwy-eet?"

His smile is replaced by a frown of confusion. I try not to gag on his cologne.

"Dwight," I repeat. "I'm named after my father's college roommate from SMU."

"*¿What's your papa's name?*" he asks in Spanish.

He's busy pulling keys from a giant ring to unlock the library doors.

"Hector," I say. Then I decide I want him to know who he's dealing with. "Hector Salazar."

Mentioning my father's name doesn't produce the desired effect. As he steps into the building, the old man starts giggling. By the time he's flipping the appropriate switches to turn off the alarm, he's cackling.

"*Lo siento mucho,*" he says as he catches his breath.

"It's the European pronunciation," I tell him, not really expecting him to understand.

"Muchacho, hate to tell jou, but jou brown. Jou got black hair. Jou got brown eyes. Only ting Jour'pean is when jou eat french fries."

He's enjoying himself. He's bracing himself with one hand on my shoulder. The other hand is holding on to his watermelon gut.

He's not worth explaining this to, but I know the old dude's wrong. Dad paid a bundle to have the family's genealogy traced by this company in Barcelona. I remember how excited he was when the packet of information arrived, because they said we were descended from some nobles over there. We were counts and countesses or something. He had the family tree framed, and he hung it in his study. Back when I was in third grade, he paid me ten dollars to memorize it. It was easy. I'm good with names and dates. At parties, he would pretend to forget some bit of biographical data, so he'd quiz me in front of our guests. His favorite one to ask about was Juan

Hector Salazar, a conquistador who came over with Cortés and conquered the Aztecs.

Dad became obsessed. He actually flew over to Spain and visited the village where we were supposed to have ruled or whatever. He came back and informed Mom and Courtney and me that we'd been saying our name wrong for generations. He instructed us in the new pronunciation and made us promise to correct all those who got it wrong. The first time I was tested was when I returned to school that fall. My first-period teacher called my name off her roll sheet.

"Salazar, Dwight?"

"That's Salazar, ma'am," I said. The room got dead silent. They'd been calling me that name since I transferred to Davy Crockett Junior High when we moved to Deerfield.

"Excuse me?" said the teacher.

"It's Salazar."

I remembered the way Dad explained it to us.

"It rhymes with *the laser.*"

And that's how I got my nickname. No one thinks much about it anymore. Except when I have to tell new people. Especially Hispanics. Some get mad. My grampa on my mother's side refuses to say it any way but the Mexican way. Dad's given up on trying to make him change.

Weedy isn't disturbed by it so much. He just thinks it's funny.

"Let's just get to work," I say as I plop down at the first table and glance at the clock. We're fifteen minutes late getting started. Fine with me. "What do you have there?" I say, pointing at what appears to be a manual he's been carrying.

He sets it down on the table.

DEERFIELD INDEPENDENT SCHOOL DISTRICT
Methods and Operations Manual

"I need to know all of this," he says, still in Spanish.

"¿Por qué?" I say, forgetting I'm supposed to be tutoring him in English.

"Because they pay manager's salary and they get insurance for their whole family. Plus they get paid for the summer."

"So?" I say, remember to use English. He switches as well.

"So, jou gotta pass test—in English—to be manager. If jou not a manager, jou hired on . . . *¿cómo se dice?* . . . contract."

Weedy's accent is strong, but no stronger than Grampa's, and Grampa can read and write in English almost as well as in Spanish. The only reason Courtney and I know any Spanish at all is because it's the only language he and Gramma would speak to us when we'd go to stay with them during the summers or when Mom and Dad went on vacations.

I slide the manual toward me. It's nearly a hundred pages and it's divided into nine sections.

"All right then. Let's take three sections each week."

"Sí."

"In English," I say.

"Hokey dokey."

The old man takes a look down at the page, looks back up at me, then attempts to sound out the first word. *"W . . . Wee . . . weel . . . weelcomb . . . "*

"Welcome," I say.

That's how it goes for the next two hours. Word by word we plug away at the introduction of the DISD employee manual. It's full of terminology that makes it sound like Dad had a hand in writing it. Even after I tell Weedy the word in English, he doesn't know what it means. I have to define it in simple Spanish, and my Spanish being what it is, that's not easy. We get to the end of the section, and Weedy reads the final word proudly.

"Huly," he says.

"July."

Weedy grins. He seems undaunted, even though we haven't exactly been cruising through the material. Now comes the part I'm worried about.

"Mr. Escobar can you tell me what this page said?"

"I just did!"

"Try putting it in your own words."

The smile that's seemed glued to Weedy's face finally starts to fade. I don't know why, but that somehow makes me happy.

"They gonna make me do that?"

"They want you to know what the manual says. All the policies and procedures. They're not just going to ask you to read it out loud."

"Why can't they just write the manual in Spanish. Then I could learn it."

I've been wondering that myself.

"Because," says my father without looking up from his folder, "this is an English-speaking country. We insist on our students speaking English, so why shouldn't we insist our faculty and staff do as well?"

"But he's a groundskeeper," I say. "It's not like he's applying for your job."

"If he's content to stay a groundskeeper, that's fine. He can speak pig latin as far as I'm concerned. The test is given—stand up straight, quit slouching—to employees who are interested in management positions. Managers have to fill out reports. They have to post schedules, Dwight. What happens when I send a memo to maintenance instructing them to keep the classrooms at eighty-five degrees instead of seventy-eight degrees, but the maintenance manager can't read English?"

Comfortable students are able to concentrate, resulting in improved achievement scores, I think to myself. *The town throws a parade in the superintendent's honor.*

"Do you know what kind of cooling bill that would result in?" my father says, answering his own question.

I see Weedy a couple of days later. He's under a tree leaning on his Weed Eater, he's got on his jumpsuit and what I now know—after reading Chapter Two, "Dress Code"—to be a nonregulation Texas

Rangers baseball cap. He's got his head buried in the district manual. I've always thought our maintenance people were kind of lazy, but one of the other things I learned in going through the manual is that they're *supposed* to turn off their equipment between classes. That's why you never see them working. The district doesn't want to get sued if a lawn mower throws a rock and puts a student's eye out

Weedy looks up and spots me. He whistles between his fingers and waves me over.

"Come on, Hectorcito, I want to show you something."

I walk over toward the tree, but I'm concerned about the time. We have six minutes for passing periods, and every tardy I get is a night I'm grounded.

"In English," I tell him when I get close enough that I don't have to shout.

"Jou see this?" he says. He hands me the manual open to a page headed "Comp Days and Vacation Days."

"Okay, what?" I say.

"That say I gonna get ten days' vacation I can use anytime. I also get ten days of sickness."

"Ten sick days," I say.

"Sí . . . jes."

Notes in pidgin Spanish are scribbled all over the page I'm looking at. I flip the page. The notes stop about a third of the way down.

"I stay up all night. Sunday and Monday."

"That's good. You know you'll have to write your answer in English."

Even as I'm saying it, I'm thinking about his chances. He's stayed up two nights, and he hasn't completed two pages. The test is in three weeks. He'd need three months to even have a small shot. But that's his problem, not mine. I just owe two more Sundays.

"Wait a minute," Weedy says. "I got something for jou. Mrs. Escobar make it for jou. To thank jou."

The old man grabs a paper sack out of a duffel bag. Waxed paper corners stick out of the top.

"Tamales," he says.

Gross, unmentionable meats smothered in greasy cornmeal and wrapped in corn husks.

"Uh, thanks."

I make sure I hold the sack away from my nose and throw it in a big trash can as soon as I round the corner of the next building.

Mr. Escobar is waiting for me outside my trig class on Thursday.

"Hectorcito," he says.

I glance around and make sure nobody heard him. "It's Dwight."

Weedy isn't smiling this time. He looks unable to. Big black bags hang from his eyes. He hands me a piece of paper. On it are words: *calculating, summary, disability, deductible.* And a bunch more.

"*¿Could you write down what these mean in Spanish for me?*"

He looks so pitiful that I don't bother to make him speak English.

"Let me see the manual."

Weedy hands it to me. He looks kind of embarrassed. I can tell by his notes he's worked his way through two more pages.

"Sure, I'll get them to you by the end of the day."

"Jou save my life," he says.

Dad keeps all the computer games loaded onto the computer in his office. That way it's easy for him to monitor my study time. Besides, he's a closet PGA Golf fan. He'll close the doors and sit in here for hours thinking I don't know what he's up to. I like the games where you get to splatter monster guts against the walls of dungeons. I'm wiping orc brain off my broadsword when I notice the district manual resting across the vastness that is my father's desk. It makes me think of Weedy at home tonight, slugging down coffee and trying to make sense of the thing one word at a time. Why doesn't he just blow it off? Do himself a favor. My virtual hero's scream snaps me out of my thoughts. While my attention was elsewhere, a troll clubbed him into submission.

I pause the game and pick up the manual. Helping out Weedy won't take that much effort. If it's one thing I do know—it's how to figure out what they're going to test you on.

By Sunday, Weedy looks like hell, but he manages to smile at me as he unlocks the library door. It's obvious he didn't go to church this Sunday. He's in sweatpants and a plain white tank-top undershirt. No cologne smell. Just B.O. and cigarettes.

"Buenos días, Hectorcito," he says.

"Yeah," I say.

He flips on the lights and shuts off the alarm. I sit down at a large table and pull out a legal pad from my folder.

"New plan," I tell Weedy. "No more reading the manual. You can throw the thing away."

"Jou crazy?"

"I've got a better way of getting you ready for the test."

Weedy doesn't look happy.

"Jou mean I crap away all that time?"

"Not completely," I say. "This'll just let you go a lot faster."

I slide the paper across the table.

"More big fancy English," he says.

"It's a test."

"Jou steal the test?" Weedy says with a hint of disapproval.

Jou wish, I think to myself.

"No. I wrote this test." Weedy looks confused. "I read the manual and figured out what they would test you on—the stuff that would really matter. Where they post memos. When time sheets are due. How to file for workmen's comp. That sort of stuff."

Weedy looks over the page in the same mystified way I do when handed a Latin exam.

"It's a hundred questions," I say. "If you can answer these, you can pass the test."

❖ ❖ ❖

I thought it would be easy. Figure out the questions. Figure out the answers. But that wasn't really Weedy's problem. It was the English. We still had to go through the questions one by one, make sure he understood what he was being asked. Then he had to form in English the answer that I provided. I told him to use the simplest words he could. I prayed spelling wouldn't count. We averaged about two questions per hour. Unfortunately, he wasn't nearly as fast at home without me. I began writing down the answers for him in Spanish, so that all he had to do was translate into English. He was still lucky to get through two or three a night on his own.

On Friday I saw him resting beneath his usual tree. He waved me over. "Present for the teacher," he said.

I'm afraid he'll pull a chalupa out his bag. Instead, he withdraws a rolled poster.

"Check it out," he says.

I roll the rubber band off one end and unfurl it. The first thing I see at the bottom is an ad for Butterkrust Bread "as American as baseball" it says. Further unrolling reveals Texas Ranger All-Stars Ivan Rodriguez and Juan Gonzalez. There are already tack holes in all four corners. I'm not really a baseball fan, but I shoot for sincerity in thanking him.

"Jou don't get no better than those two," says Weedy. "EYE-van ROD-ri-gwez and Johnny GON-ze-lez."

"Look," I say angrily. "Back in Spain—"

But Weedy's chuckling cuts me short.

"I just give jou a hard time, muchacho. Don't jou *ever* laugh?"

Weedy reaches out and tousles my hair like I'm ten or something.

There was a PTA meeting scheduled in the library this afternoon, so I agreed to meet with Weedy at his house. It was either his or mine, so . . . you know. Weedy's house is in the middle of what they call Little Matamoras—row after row of tiny wooden houses with front porches that always seem to slope danger-ously off to one side, a.c. units filling windows. Nobody has central air. I happen to know I'd die without central air. When I pulled up, I noticed the Escobar house is one of the few that doesn't have even one Montgomery Ward "Cool Zone II" gurgling away out a window. I guess they just suffer.

Mrs. Escobar lets me in the house. She takes me through a tiny living room, stopping to point out pho-tographs of her children and tell me all about them. The photos are framed and hanging above a shelf that holds up three or four candles with the Virgin Mary painted on the side. The way the photos are arranged in a pyramid sort of reminds me of the way Dad's geneaology tree looks above his desk. As I'm check-ing the photos out, Mrs. Escobar narrates. I learn that Raphael, pictured in a Deerfield baseball letter jacket, is in the army. He's stationed in Virginia. Letty is married and living a few blocks away. She doesn't say much about Antonio, who I notice is the only one not photographed in a graduation gown. Mrs. Escobar is speaking very quickly in Spanish, and I'm having a little trouble keeping up, but I think she's telling me that Carlos is going to Texas A&I down in Kingsville and living with a sister of hers.

"*¡Tuition costs so much!*" she says.

I notice a stand across from a tattered Easy Boy where a square space free of dust makes it obvious that a TV used to go in that spot. Weedy is sitting in the next room in a T-shirt and sweatpants. He's smoking a cigarette, and he's got the practice test out on the kitchen table. He looks up at me.

"Thank you for calling Deerfield Public Schools. How can I be of assistance?"

He says it like he's a game show announcer. Then laughs. It's the line he's supposed to deliver when he answers a district telephone . . . once he's a manager. That tells me he's made it at least to question fifty. Fifty-six to be exact.

Hours later, we're on question seventy-nine of my practice test. What's weird is that I've sort of lost track of time. Weedy's drinking coffee, and Mrs. Escobar keeps pouring me Albertson's cola, so we're both riding caffeine buzzes. We're still going pretty slowly, but for the first time I think we can both sort of imagine getting to the end. It's the weirdest thing, but when Weedy gets an answer right, I'm getting a thrill out of it. I realize his passing this test does me no good in the long run, but I've always sort of liked contests and that's how this sort of feels to me except that, at first, I can't figure out who we're competing against. I laugh out loud when the answer pops into my head. About the same time, my electronic leash starts beeping. I check the liquid crystal display, knowing before I do that it's my father. My English test is in the morning—a fact he's well aware of. He actually taped the Hill Country Prep brochure to the bathroom door so I'd be sure to see it this morning. He didn't stop me from coming over to Weedy's, but that's because it would look bad if he did—the community service requirement was sort of his pet project. I remember him getting up in front of the school board, his voice booming like it does.

"It's time for the students of Lee High School to give something back to Deerfield!"

I check my watch. My community service requirement was complete two hours ago.

"*¿What's this word?*"

I've given up on making Weedy speak English.

"Deductible—remember? *It's how much of the doctor bill you have to pay.*"

He gets right back to work. He makes it through that question and another before I tell him I have to leave. He looks up, sort of surprised. Then he glances across a clock that reads nine o' clock and sighs.

"Hokey dokey," he says.

I drive a few blocks toward the highway and pull

over at the pay phone in front of the Sac-N-Pac. I dial home. My father answers.

"It's me," I say.

"I assume you're studying."

"Gonna pull an all-nighter at a friend's. I'll be home in the morning to shower."

"Dedication pays off. You'll see."

Weedy's suprised to see me back on his front porch. I'm carrying a big bag of Ruffles and a six-pack of Mountain Dew.

"All-nighter supplies," I tell him.

By midnight we're pretty wiped out. I can just barely keep my eyes open. I think I even fall asleep a couple times with my head on the table. Each new question is taking us about twenty minutes. Mrs. Escobar hands us each a squirt bottle from under the sink.

"Agua," she says. "If the other sleeps."

I spray Weedy once just to make sure my bottle works.

We finish the test at about two-thirty. Both our shirts are wet from spraying each other so much. I've only got one Mountain Dew left. The Ruffles have been gone for an hour. Weedy gets up and turns the Spanish radio station on low. It's almost like he planned it—they're playing the Macarena. He breaks right into the dance. He slithers his arms out, back in, behind his butt, then does one of the most vulgar hip grinds I've ever seen. I'm dying laughing.

"Let me teach jou," he says.

I'm so delirious, I do it. I stand across from him and use him like a mirror. By the time the song ends, it's official. Now *everyone* in America knows this stupid dance.

Even though we've gotten all the way through the questions, we decide that's not enough. Weedy needs to be able to remember the answers. He gets out a flashlight, hands it to me, and the two of us walk around Little Matamoros. I read out questions, he gives me answers. Moving this way, we're able to stay alert a little better. I have to prompt Weedy a lot. He doesn't have all the English down like he should, but we're getting there.

It's five in the morning when we get back to the house. I'm still pretty delirious. When I try to sit, I miss the chair. I'm flat on my back, laughing again. The radio is still playing, but the Latin hip-hop is gone. They're playing the oldies. I can't believe I actually know the song that's playing. *"Quatro Milpas."* Gramma and Grampa used to play it all the time. They told me it was the first dance at their wedding.

Cuatro milpas tan solo tan quedado en el rancho que era mie, ai, ai, ai, ai . . . "

It's about how all that's left of the old family farm is four cornfields.

Still on my back, I begin singing along.

"Aquella casita tan blanca y bonita tan triste que esta . . ."

And a little white deserted house . . .

My eyes start getting all watery. The song is so

sad, but it makes me happy for some reason. The funny thing is, I'm pretty sure I know why. It reminds me of summers. Before high school. Before Gramma died. When Courtney and I would go stay with Gramma and Grampa down in the Rio Grande Valley. They'd walk us through the fields and the orchards where they used to pick fruit and vegetables. Tell us funny stories about our mother. Tell us how much better it was growing up in America than in Mexico. About how if you worked hard, blistered your hands in the fields each day, you could make a better life. Save your money and you could send your child to college.

Tan triste que esta . . .

It's still dark when Mrs. Escobar gets up. She's stands in front of the stove cooking. She brews a new pot of coffee. Weedy pours himself a cup and walks me out to the front porch.

"How do jou do good on tests?" he asks as he sits in one of the two molded plastic lawn chairs.

"Don't panic," I say.

We sit there facing east as the sun comes up. Mrs. Escobar brings us each a plate of migas and tortillas. I didn't know eggs could taste this good.

"Dr. Salazar will see you now," says my father's secretary.

I stand and rake my fingers through my hair.

"Come on in, Dwight," my father coaxes.

I enter and stand in front of his desk. He's got a

stern look on his face, but my father is a terrible actor. I let him play out his scene anyway.

"I had a little chat with Mrs. Paulson," he says. He tries to sound like a TV cop in an interrogation room. "She was kind enough to grade your test during her conference period today."

Kind? Fearful, maybe.

"Yes, sir."

"Frankly, there's no way I can sugarcoat this . . . "

This is the part where he lets a smile start to sneak out.

"You made a ninety-two. Congratulations. Mrs. Paulson said there was a marked improvement in your essay question answers."

He sticks his hand out across the desk, and we shake. He reaches into his wallet and pulls out a ten-dollar bill.

"Why don't you have some fun tonight? Go see a movie or something."

"Thank you," I say, pocketing the ten. *Great, a movie by myself on a Monday night.* "Hey, Dad, do you know if anyone passed the district management test today?"

"No one passed," he says. "Your old groundskeeper showed up to take it, but he missed it by a few points."

"Can people take it as many times as they want?"

"Yes, of course. We give it twice a year."

I nod, then turn to leave.

"Dwight?" he says sharply.

I stop and look back at him.

"Get those shoes of yours shined."

"Yes, sir."

"Oh, and Dwight?"

I wait.

"Did you learn a little something about hard work?"

For a moment I'm tempted to tell how I didn't study at all. Instead, I just answer his question.

"*Sí,*" I say, and close the door behind me.

Ten Pins Down

The ten pin is the only one left standing. I'm positioned next to the ball return, dangling my fingers in the fan. Satisfied, I take a step to the right, bring the ball up to my chest, take a deep breath, and stare down the alley. As I exhale, I let all my thoughts drain until I reach my "crystal pool." Following the instructions of the sports psychologist they hired for the football team after we lost three straight, I visualize the ball hurtling down the alley . . . clipping the pin . . . sending it flying . . . enticing Nadia to scream . . . prompting her to hug . . . causing Ben to shit . . . elevating me to —

"I don't know how he can use that fourteen-pounder," announces Ben, muddying up my pool. "Ball's too light for me. It's like a little kid's ball or something. I could probably throw it overhand."

I don't turn around, but Ben's toady yes-man Phil laughs like what Ben said is actually funny. I wish I could just glance over and see what Nadia's reaction is. Is it possible she's impressed? Surely she sees through his weak-ass bullshit? Does she know you get better control from the lighter balls? Is the ten pin always this close to the gutter?

Hell with the crystal pool. Three steps and I let 'er rip. I throw not so much for score, but for power. The ball takes two hard bounces, then steams thunderously down the lane, smacking the back mat two feet to the left of the pin.

"Tough luck, pal," Ben says with enough fake sincerity that I want to rip his face off. Besides, *he* knows that *I* know that when he says "pal," he's *thinking* personal ass licker. We've both been aware of that fact since second grade.

Second grade was the year our parents became friends, the same year the Lions Club Kick starring Grant Ehlam and Ben Shrank won the greater Deerfield soccer championship. But Little League, being what it is, only allowed one player from each team to make the all-star squad. My dad coached the Kick, and he picked Ben despite the fact that I led the team in assists and was second to Ben in goals scored. Not to mention I was his only son. Apparently being a team player was supposed to be its own reward. I haven't played soccer since. Ben kept playing, and he's currently leading our high school to a nearly-inevitable district championship. State isn't out the question.

Rah.

I played football, instead, which, looking back, may have been a big mistake. I was second-string quarterback throughout junior high, as a freshman, as a sophomore, the first six games of my senior year. The best four months of my life were when I was the starting JV quarterback my junior year.

Everyone makes the mistake of thinking Ben and I are friends. I guess it's understandable. Since our parents have stayed friends, we've had to go on ski trips to Colorado together (where I kicked his ass, even though he swore he wasn't racing me). Our families hit Wet-N-Wild at least twice a summer. Neither Ben or I got a vote when the people who gave us birth went in on a speedboat together. Technically we alternate weekends, but what always happens is that the families go together and we're forced to watch Ben ski barefoot. If I had size fourteens and webbed toes, maybe I could do it too. But the worst result of this midlife bonding is that Ben and I have to carpool together. Each family has two cars and they alternate the weeks that Ben and I are allowed to take one to school. Part of the deal is that we have to drop our sisters off at the junior high. They even get along great.

Ben and I are both picking up our community service hours "à la carte." A few hours here collecting city council election campaign signs. A few hours there scraping grackle droppings off the town square sidewalks. We're getting twenty-four this weekend participating in the Stamp Out Cancer Bowlathon. They'll actually double your hours if you collect more than two hundred dollars in pledges. I wrested fifty cents a game from my parents after I told them that's what Ben's parents donated. I got another quarter a game from my grandparents on my dad's side and a reluctant nickel from Mom's mom. That means I only need to get in about five hundred games to collect two hundred dollars. We've been at it for seventeen hours and I've bowled sixteen games; I'm hardly dipping into my inheritance. The organizers have you bowl for two hours, then take two hours off, but we're locked in here at Sunset Lanes, so we can't go anywhere. They've turned the bar into a lights-out sleeping area with cots and pillows and stuff, but I've had enough Mountain Dew (free to bowlers!) that I think I'll still be awake a week from Wednesday. If I don't get too tired from pissing before then.

"A nine. *Très bien*," says Nadia.

"Thanks," I say.

"Yeah, a nine's not bad," says Ben.

I give him the bird.

My partner is Gina Gresser, whose family always hosts a foreign exchange student. Nadia is this year's model from Belgium. Keeping team scores has been kind of pointless. Ben and I have been switching out partners, but whichever team Gina's on wins. She's consistently bowling about a hundred pins higher than Nadia, who's averaging in the high teens. Don't get me wrong—she's looking damn fine doing it. The provocative way she scrunches up her face, bites her lip, and shakes her head after a gutter ball . . . dark bangs falling

in front of her face . . . old jeans fitting tight . . . top two
buttons of her blouse flapping . . . umm, umm, umm.

Gina rolls her third strike of the game. I start
chanting.

"U-S-A! U-S-A!"

Gina does a perky Olympic gymnast wave to an
imaginary audience. She's cool.

"I'd like to apologize on behalf of the United
States," Ben says to Nadia.

See. It's that sort of thing that drives me nuts. I'll
tell you what. Ben and I have completely different
strategies when it comes to the ladies. He's all com-
plimentary—"Those sure are nice earrings." "What's
that perfume you're wearing? Wow." Or my favorite,
"You've got a really nice smile."

Please.

I take a different approach. The cool approach. I
don't hang all over a girl or tell her she's the most
beautiful creature to illuminate the dark corners of
Planet Earth like Ben does. I maintain a certain man-
liness, try not to look *too* interested. I know she's
there. She knows I know she's there. If she likes what
she sees, maybe we can work something out.

Ben doesn't mean it as a tribute when he calls me
The Fonz.

The thing is, we've seen each other in action so
much, and so many times in pursuit of the same
woman, that I think it's when we hate each other
the most.

"I've heard Brussels is a beautiful city," Ben tells

Nadia as she waits for her first gutter ball to be returned. "You'll have to show me around if I ever make it over there."

"Yeah, and could you bring me home a waffle?" I say.

Gina snickers. Phil, who's supposed to be on his hour-long nap break, sneers and walks off. *Gee, I'll miss him.*

You know another thing I hate about Ben? He can grow a full beard in about three days. *That* doesn't bother me so much, because men with beards look either like Bible study leaders or somebody's dad. But, after seventeen hours of bowling, he's got this even field of stubble that I've got to admit nails a certain Marlboro Boy look. The dickhead can't drive a standard, but he somehow manages to pull off ruggedness.

We're in our final frame of game seventeen and Ben's the last bowler. That last open frame gave me a 176. Ben's coming off another split eight. What does he expect? Rolling that oversized shot put down there with no spin. Of course he ends up with splits. He has no bowling savvy whatsoever. He just lines the ball up with the middle arrow of the lane and powers it straight down like it's an animated geometry proof. Even his bowling lacks personality. He's twenty-seven pins back with a 149, but his first two balls are strikes. After that he's seven pins back with his bonus frame left to roll. We've each won eight of our first sixteen games, but who's counting?

I fill in the little block that's projected up on the screen above us. Ben tilts his head back. His lips move as he does the calculations. I want to mention this phenomenon to someone—Nadia, particularly—but I'm afraid she wouldn't get it, and it's the sort of thing that isn't funny if you have to explain it.

"Don't forget to carry the one," I say just loud enough for Ben to hear me.

He surreptitiously grabs his dick.

Then he stares down the alley and begins his approach. He releases the ball, but doesn't bother to watch it. Instead he turns, smirks, and does this John Travolta strut back toward me. His ball crushes the one pin dead square and pins start flying.

"Add that, Fonz," he says, allowing his smirk to blossom into a shit-eating grin.

The seven and ten are still standing. The rat bastard just got the eight pins he needed to beat me.

"My life is over," I tell him as deadpan as I can get. "I can't go on. Guess my team'll just have to settle for our ninety-four pin victory."

He nods and continues to grin. He knows I'm full of shit—the team score didn't matter to either of us.

Just as Ben is collecting a hug from Nadia, one of the sponsors of the Bowlathon comes on the intercom and tells us it's time to rotate. For our group that means it's break time.

"Fries?" Ben asks Nadia.

"Sure," I say.

"Well, then, you could get us some, too," says Ben

reaching his arm around the bench where he and Nadia are sitting. I shake my head as his hand reappears on the other side of her—not touching, but it's just a matter of time.

"All this testosterone," Gina says, waving her hand in front of her nose like it's a bad odor.

"I've had it," I say. Now that I'm out of the Nadia scamarama, I realize how tired I am. I don't even have to fake a yawn. "Wake me up when it's time to wipe out leukemia."

Without bothering to change out of my blue and orange bowling shoes, I trudge off to the nap room. Inside, bowlers are standing, stretching and wiping gunk out of their eyes to get ready for their two-hour slot. I nab the cot that's furthest from the door, behind the pool table, tucked into the darkest corner of the lounge. The last person out pulls the string on the Bud Light sign, and I'm in nearly total darkness, a glowing jukebox across the room providing the only remaining light. My body's had it. My neck muscles keep going on strike—refusing to keep my head upright. I can't stop yawning—I didn't try to stockpile sleep before coming like everyone else—but now that I'm lying down the caffeine from the sodas keeps forcing my eyes to pop open.

This is hell. I roll over onto my stomach. Light fills the room momentarily, then it's dark again.

"Grhont?"

The voice is female. The accent . . . French!

"Over here," I say.

My eyes are used to the dark. I can see her form move through the lounge.

"Watch the . . . "

She runs her shin into an empty cot.

"Sheet."

" . . . cot. Okay, you're clear," I say as she stumbles left. "Take three steps forward . . . all right . . . Now, turn right and take three steps toward my voice."

She's standing above me.

"Bingo," I say.

Nadia reaches down blindly. One of her hands lands on my face, the other on my stomach, dangerously close to the fun zone.

"I can see nozzing," she says without moving her hands.

"What happened to Ben?" I ask.

"Why? Do you meess heem? Do you want me to go find heem for you?"

Nadia straightens like she's going to leave, but I manage to grab one of her wrists.

"What'd you come in here for, anyw—?"

But Nadia's kissing me before I can finish my question. At first it's unbelievable. She throws a leg over the other side of the cot and straddles me. We're grinding and making out. I'm composing my *Penthouse* Forum letter in my head.

I never thought these stories were true!

She's got her hands up my shirt, and her tongue's taking inventory of my teeth. But something tastes nasty. *Gross.* She's been smoking. So that's why she kept going to "les femmes." I pull my head back and try to make it seem like I'm doing it so I can work on her ear. I start nibbling the lobe and flicking my tongue inside. She makes some breathy sound and claws at my chest, but her hair smells like cigarettes too.

Light floods into the lounge. A figure lingers in the doorway. Tall. Wearing shorts. I recognize the cut of the "stressed" denim Calvins, the kind that sweat-shop workers in Sri Lanka mutilate with bricks and cheese graters. It's Ben. I'm watching his silhouette over Nadia's shoulder. Neither her hands nor her hips show any signs of slowing. I return my mouth to her ear and she lets out a sigh. The light dims in the room as the door eases closed.

Make like a tree, Potsey.

And we're alone again.

The interruption has given me time to assess my situation. I check the facts:

1. A beautiful foreign exchange student seems ready to swap bodily fluids with me.

2. Ben is outside ordering a snow cone.

So what if she smokes? I think I heard somewhere that they all do in Europe. I think it's because their air is so crappy already, they figure it can't hurt. Keeping this in mind, I start unbuttoning Nadia's blouse. I'm kinda freaked about the way she's been letting her fingers do the walking—that's my job. Whatever the French word is for *no*, I don't hear it. I pull the blouse back over Nadia's shoulders. She responds by lifting my shirt up, but I keep her from pulling it over my head. I mean, someone else *could* walk in. I'm kissing down her neck, then down to her shoulder. There's a minor glitch in the rhythm when I land on the Jesus Lizard tattoo she's got on her shoulder, but I refuse to let myself think about it too much.

By now Nadia's talking. But it's in French. Her eyes are closed, and she's still dealing out the friction, so, naturally, I assume whatever she's saying doesn't require an answer. She's somewhere between a *frère* and a *Jacques* when I spot it.

Twin patches of long . . . silky . . . brown . . . man-like . . . pit pubes.

Holy mother of —

"Damn it," I say.

"What?"

"Jeremy Wallace—I promised I'd fill in for him during his break. They're letting him out to do his paper route this morning. I'll bet they're looking for me."

"They don't find you so far," says little miss body hair.

"Yeah, we're lucky."

I pull down my shirt and twist out from under her.

"Sorry about this," I say as I squeeze her hand and weave my way through the cocktail table obstacle course toward the light. The bowlathon has managed to persevere without me, and there's something refreshing about the sound of pins and balls smashing together.

I wander into the arcade, which is full of bowlers

on break. Maybe the cancer people would have been better off if we'd just given them the money we'll end up spending on NBA Jam over the course of the night. Ben is in the corner playing Pop-A-Shot. Naturally Phil is cheering him on. When I get over there, Ben is into bonus time. He's shooting with whichever hand is able to grab the next miniature basketball, trying to get off as many shots as possible. That's one school of thought; it's not the way I'd do it.

His last three shots clang off the rim.

"Sorry son," says Ben as he punches in his initials (B. S.—Hah!) for the new high score. "I don't give lessons."

I pull a ten-dollar bill out of my wallet and wake up the lackey they have manning the arcade booth. I slide the bill across the counter.

"Give me a roll of quarters," I say.

High score, my ass.

Turtles

"You want me to do what?"

I musta heard Miss Amenny wrong, cuz the lady's known me too long to ask me somethin' like that.

"You heard me, Tommy."

"Naw, I couldn't have, cuz what I thought you said was that you wanted me to direct a bunch of juvenile delinquents in a play."

Miss A smiles at me like she does.

"I didn't say juvenile delinquents, Tommy. I said kids from the junior high At Risk Program."

"Like I said—juvies. Look, I was one of them. I know what they're like. They're bicycle thiefs. Gangster wannabes. Bucket-headed dolts. Twelve-year-old alcoholics."

"Dolts?"

"It's what Dr. Doom calls the Thing."

"Which were you?" she asks as she reaches for her decaf.

I sip on my coffee while I decide.

"None of 'em, I guess. The jester, maybe."

"I didn't know jesters could still find work."

"Didn't say it paid well," I say. "Look, I thought you said I could direct the faculty play."

"I said I'd consider you, Tommy, but Gil and Rainy have both been in drama for four years. This is only your fifth semester. Besides, I think you'll appreciate what I'm going to do for you."

"What? Fly the flag at half-mast the day one of them carves me up with a switchblade?"

"I got permission for you to use this play as your community service project."

"I was really looking forward to cleaning bedpans down at County General."

"Quit chasing pipe dreams, Tommy. This is real life."

Miss A makes me laugh. Direct a kiddie play with a cast of junior high riffraff? Hmmm. I could do something simple . . . *Three Little Pigs* or the like. Perform it once for their school. The audience'll be so out of control, so happy to be out of class, no one'll even hear it. The principal and teachers will be completely embarrassed by the conduct, they'll apologize and tell me what a fine job I did.

"I'll do it," I say.

"One more thing," she says.

"Yeah?"

"You'll be taking the play on the road."

"Where," I say, feeling a willie start to creep up my spine.

"The Texas Renaissance Festival," she says. "They wanted a children's play. I volunteered yours."

I'm a success story.

I learn this on the first day I go to meet the puberty-challenged thespians I'll be directing. It's how Mrs. Doyle, who's been running the At Risk Program since way before I got to junior high, introduces me to my troupe.

"This is Tommy Parks," she says to the group. "He's one of our success stories."

Let's see. I make a quarter more than minimum wage at Whataburger. I'm gonna graduate in three months ranked 272 in a class of 310. I don't even have a beeper. Nothing about me's gonna impress this group. Hell, I'm not all that impressed.

But look what I'm competing against. One of the guys who went through the At Risk program in junior high with me is in Huntsville, and I don't mean he's enrolled in humanities classes at Sam Houston State. He's eligible for parole after three consecutive ninety-nine-year terms. Another At Risk compadre of mine has been working full-time at the fish hatchery since he dropped out. I'm not sure which of them has it worse.

"I'm the bad guy," says a kid in the back row, who's wearing sunglasses and a Zig Zag rolling papers T-shirt. Some teacher must have made him put masking tape over the logo, but the spiky leaves are poking out where the tape's starting to peel.

"I am the Antichrist," I say, one-upping the kid.

"No, fag. The bad guy . . . in the play."

And that starts a fight, because all the kids in there—even the girls—want to be the bad guy in the play. I haven't even chosen what we're doing yet.

"Ashley, you watch your language," warns Mrs. Doyle.

Ashley?

My stepfather, Dan, leads me through Thermon's football field-sized windowless, metal warehouse. Human-sized wooden spools of heat-traced tubing are stacked fifteen feet high in a web of aisles. Dudes are zipping around in little forklifts, moving spools from the third shelf on one aisle to the second shelf two aisles down for no reason I can see. All the spools look the same to me, but Dan tells me how shipping a spool of XRQ11.4 instead of a spool of XPQ11.4 is the sort of thing that gets a guy sent back to production.

"Production?"

"You'll see," says Dan.

One of the forklifts honks at us. Dan waves. It's Albert Hayes, who lives two trailers down from us in Tornado Bait Park, the absolute swankiest of all Deerfield's mobile home "communities." I don't care what the people at the Lightning Rod Villas say.

"Showing the boy the ropes?" Albert says.

"He wishes. I'm about to take him to production."

Albert laughs.

"One thousand, three hundred ten," says Albert.

"Three thousand, nine hundred sixty-four," says Dan.

Albert says, "Time flies" as he zips away. I continue to watch him as he lowers his spool of TYU-556 onto shelf one of Aisle NN.

"What did he—"

"Days till retirement," says Dan before I can get the question all the way out of my mouth.

Dan and I exit the warehouse through a set of double-steel doors. We walk through a little shrub-happy courtyard ringed with vending machines. I recognize a couple guys standing by a cigarette machine who were seniors when I was a freshman. One's smoking, other one's dipping. Both have packed on thirty-pound rolls of flab since graduation.

"Here it is," says Dan as we get to another set of doors.

I've figured this was my destiny for so long that it seems like the doors ought to be fancier than these flat gray ones in front of me. Maybe I was expecting a doorman who would hand me a beer, a car payment booklet, and a lease for my new efficiency apartment. Instead, I'm welcomed by two signs: NO SMOKING and AFTER 9 P.M. ALARM WILL SOUND.

Once I'm inside, I can't decide which one of my senses suffers most. The hard black plastic they use to encase the tubing is simmering in gargantuan black witches' cauldrons. A little eye of newt might actually improve the bouquet. Within seconds of walking along one of the catwalks, I feel like I've got a second skin of fiberglass fibers, the kind they use to insulate the tubing. I make the mistake of rubbing my eyes, and everything else I view looks like it's on the other side of a waterfall. One-time Lee Rebels wearing jumpsuits, goggles, and earplugs take their time unloading semis. There seems to be at least one truck in reverse at all times—a fact brought home by the piercing, monotonous beeps that ring against the complex's sheet-metal walls.

"*This* is production," Dan shouts.

Good thing he cleared that up for me. I was beginning to think the trough of melted plastic running from vat to vat was the River Styx.

Dan leads me up to a glassed-in office space that overlooks the factory floor. There he asks a paper clip sculptor if we can see the Chuckster. She pages by, yelling, "Chuck! Fresh meat."

The Chuckster is hitching up his pants as he comes out of his office. It's plain he isn't quite used to wearing a tie. He's loosened all the way down to the second shirt button of his short-sleeved shirt. It's only ten in the morning.

"G.E.D.?" he says, apparently ready to hand me a uniform right then.

"I wish," I say. I hand him my transcript. I'm getting my name in early for the jobs that open up in the summer. They give guys who graduate fifteen cents more an hour than guys who don't.

"He's making his mama happy," says Dan, "holdin' out for that diploma."

"Good man," says the Chuckster. "Got too many dropouts down here already."

That makes both him and Dan laugh. I guess neither of them got the thrill of throwing a square cap up in the air. I stare out on the floor and wonder how many of the guys moving around down there walked the stage.

"So, did you want to start in the marketing department developing new advertising strategies, or do you want to go straight into the executive training program?"

I don't know what sort of momentary brain lock I come down with at that moment, but I stupidly let hope cross my face as I turn back to answer the Chuckster.

"Gotcha," he says, and he and Dan bust out again.

But I don't care. They can start me out there on the floor. I'll be making nearly four more dollars an hour than I am now. I'll be able to afford my own place. Something cheap, but I'll be out of the trailer. Plus, I'll get health insurance, sick leave, paid vacation, retirement.

Ten thousand more days.

I convince my cast that Robin Hood and his merry posse are all a bunch of outlaws.

"They're *stealing* from the rich," I tell them, leaving out the part about giving to the poor.

I couldn't find any decent one-act scripts for Robin Hood, so I've had to sort of make my own by cutting up all the ones I could find and pasting them back together in a new sort of Robin Hood-meets-Quentin Tarantino production that's a half hour of action, three minutes of dialogue. I do this more for my benefit than for the audience's. We have a sword fight with Will Scarlet, a quarterstaff battle with Little John, an archery contest with the Sheriff of Nottingham, and just for good measure, Friar Tuck tosses Robin into a river. I even write in a bit where Maid Marian pulls out some kung fu on a couple guards. Our version of Robin Hood isn't quite theater; it has more in common with a sports event.

There's not a single soliloquy in the script by the time I get finished with it. I just drop in a few jokes and lots of cocky one-liners.

LITTLE JOHN: *Let's see where we can stick this.*
WILL SCARLET: *Care for a slice?*
FRIAR TUCK: *Stop your wining or we'll all go to ale!*

It takes me two rehearsals to cast the show. In that time I figure out their reasons for being in the show are, for the most part, even less noble than my own: Six of the nine have been busted for a variety of crimes, and the judge handling youth offenders in Deerfield has given them the option of an extracurricular activity at school or eight consecutive Saturdays of cleaning trash on the highway. I'm thinking it might be funny to have head-on and profile mug shots in the program. We could even include their rap sheet.

Robin — Zo Roland

Miss A always told me that you put your most charismatic kid as the lead, which meant, in this case, having a brother play Robin Hood. Even though he's got Denzel looks, I was gonna cast him as a Merry Man 'cuz I thought he was a mute, but one day when rehearsal got particularly out of hand, Zo shouted, "Chill!" and the other hoodlums just zipped up. I knew at that moment, he was my man.

The crime: After a sixteen-year-old demanded his basketball shoes, Zo beat him unconscious with a two-by-four.

Maid Marian — Lissy Granberry

Our poor little rich girl. Lissy's parents are divorcing and splitting the Granberry Ready-Mix Concrete empire in half. Lissy has responded by following some "how to rebel" handbook to the letter: dyeing her hair magenta, wearing black, leaving suicide notes in can't-miss locations around the house, refusing to complete any homework (though Mrs. Doyle assured me she still aces tests), and hanging out with a "bad crowd," which, in this case, means other kids with bad haircuts.

The crime: Picked up twice by police for panhandling outside the Li'l Engine That Could Depot, where they sell tickets for the miniature steam train that takes kids through Deerfield's parks.

Little John—Dodie Saucedo
He looked like he had kicked puberty's ass around second grade. If it weren't for his full side-burns and status as the only one in the room topping six feet, I'm sure the other kids would have ragged on him for his habit of wearing puff-painted T-shirts of his own design.

The crime: Caught on tape shoplifting Armani fragrances by the Eckerd's closed circuit security system.

Will Scarlet—Thad Swiderski
I've seen a lot of white kids who liked to pretend they're brothers. Thad is the first Polack I know who's sure he's Mexican. He's got the 1940s L.A. pachuco accent. He's got the khakis so loaded with starch, they'd qualify as a school lunch item. He's got the top button of his flannel shirt buttoned. He's in one of the little junior high gangs, *Asesinitos Allegres* (The Happy Little Killers).

The crime: Spray-painting "¡No Grapes!" in six-foot-tall letters across the exterior wall of Albertson's.

Friar Tuck—Travis McGee
I didn't really have a fat kid to work with, so I went against type and got me the skinniest, paint-sniffing, Sepultura-listening, quivering little skeleton I could find. Besides, his Irish blood and rap sheet made him a natural for the part.

The crime: Passing out in Baskin-Robbins led to his fourth M.I.P. citation. Of note: He was working there at the time.

The Sheriff of Nottingham — Ashley Ford
Stoner. Bully. Thief. Liar. Neighbor.
Got the highly sought-after role when he told me
he knew where I lived.
*The crime: Taking the junior high principal's minivan
and seventh-grade daughter on an unauthorized field trip to
Five-Mile Dam.*

Mrs. Little John/Lady-in-Waiting — Ashanti White
Things Ashanti is not interested in: schoolwork,
U.S. foreign policy, this play. Things Ashanti is interested in: her hair, Toni Braxton, Zo Roland. Her desire
to play a love scene with Zo dashed by her habit of
rolling her eyes after every sentence she speaks.

Merry Man/Soldier — Phuong Ngo
Probably shouldn't be in the At Risk Program.
Most likely some lazy teacher confused not speaking
English with being stupid. He never opens his mouth,
but he's able to collapse in all three of his death scenes
with complete disregard for his own safety. Probably
didn't know why he was raising his hand when he
volunteered for the play.

Merry Man/Soldier — Daryl Berry
He can't read, or at least that's what his classmates
say. I don't have a clue why he's in the play, but I need
the extra body, and he's able to memorize, "Robin!
Watch out!"

I start driving over to the junior high during sixth period instead of doing my usual bunch of nothing as Miss Amenny's drama aide. We get about forty-five minutes together each day, but I'm lucky if I get a decent fifteen minutes of rehearsal out of 'em. The rest of the time is used up trying to get 'em to be quiet, quit giggling, stop fighting, get back in the room, and quit touching each other.

Today's a big day because I've actually got my hands on all the props: swords, bows, stick horses, quarterstaffs.

"When do we get costumes?" Ashanti asks.

"I ain't wearing tights," says Ashley for the seventeenth time in the last week.

"Costumes will be ready before a week from Wednesday," I say.

"¿Por qué?" says Thad.

"'Cuz that's when we'll be doing our first dress rehearsal," I tell him.

"I ain't wearing tights," Ashley repeats.

"No one'll see, right?" says Travis.

"No, we'll have an audience," I answer.

"But we suck," says Lissy.

"Who?" says Travis.

"Who what?"

"Who's the audience?"

"The honors English classes," I say. "Their teachers are gonna bring down their classes."

"Jackrabbits?!" Travis says with fear and disgust.

It's funny. I haven't used that word for years.

Probably not since junior high or before. It's slang for the brainiacs, the honors kids, but of course it's one you'd never use around them, 'cuz it's almost like admitting they're better than you. It all started back in elementary school. Teachers would put you in groups for reading or math, and they'd think you were too dumb to catch the drift—smart kids would be in the jackrabbit group. Your group would be turtles.

"I quit then," says Travis.

"I'll let the judge know," I say.

"Let's just do it and get it over with," says Zo.

"I ain't wearin' no tights," Ashley reminds us.

"You know what they say about men who refuse to wear tights?" I say.

"What?" snaps Ashley.

"They're ashamed of something."

The cast, except for Ashley, busts out *oohing* and *in-your-facing*. Ashley says he'd whip out right there in the gymnasium if there was enough room. For a couple minutes, we're all able to forget about the jackrabbits coming to see our play.

With a couple days left until our dress rehearsal, I've reduced my list of problems with the show down from twenty-two to ten. I put them on a note card in general order of importance.

> 1. No one even attempts to play a character. They won't let themselves

get out of themselves, so it's just Zo muttering Robin Hood's lines, Lissy smacking gum as Maid Marian, Dodie practically skipping across the stage when it's Little John's cue.

2. No one has their lines memorized. Not that it matters, because . . .

3. You can't hear anyone in the cast if you're more than three rows back in an empty theater.

4. The fight sequences boast all the fury and danger of fly-fishing.

5. My manager at Whataburger is starting to get on my ass about showing up late after rehearsal.

6. They giggle every time someone misses a line or a cue.

7. Ashley won't wear tights.

8. The police have stopped rehearsal twice so they could question Travis.

9. My Polish Will Scarlet keeps announcing that the "Chairif is shicken."

10. The longer Zo ignores Ashanti's flirting, the bigger her hair gets.

I guess my biggest problem, really, is that no one will do anything I tell them to. That makes the rest of problems pretty much uncorrectable. Early on, I blew my whistle and told everybody to listen up.

"Why should we?" said Zo. "If you're the big success

story, it don't look like we got much to look forward to."
It's tough to argue with that logic.

Miss Amenny actually comes over to the junior high for the dress rehearsal. She gets to check out firsthand what I have to deal with when I give them their costumes. You'd think they were all Norma Desmond in previous lives. They bitch about everything. All the boys think they looked like fags. The girls think the dresses make them look pregnant. As he warned us, Ashley refuses to wear the tights.

The play opens with Robin riding into Sherwood Forest on his stick horse, but Zo doesn't gallop like he's supposed to. He just does his little cool walk across the stage dragging the horse behind him. I can tell that the honors kids have been warned not to laugh, but a few titters are loud enough for anyone to hear. Watching the rest of the show is sort of like witnessing an execution performed with toenail clippers. If a line is missed, no one makes an attempt to cover.

SHERIFF: *I command you to tell me where Robin Hood went!*
FRIAR TUCK:
SHERIFF: *Watch your tongue, Friar.*

Someone screws up in the quarterstaff fight between Robin and Little John, and Zo ends up with a gash along his eyebrow that gushes blood. This unrehearsed moment gives the show its one moment of unbridled drama. It also adds a bit of slapstick as the next three characters who enter downstage right slip in the blood puddle. By now the honors kids are howling with laughter. Ashley has quit saying any of his lines; he's just staring out into the lights deciding how much trouble he'll get in if he dives out into the crowd and breaks a couple noses. I notice that as each character enters, he or she is wearing a little less costume and a little more street clothes. By the end of the play I think Phuong is the only one still ready to take on Prince John's men.

No one's really left in the audience to notice, though. Teachers began dismissing their classes by row almost ten minutes before the rescue of Maid Marian. As the last junior high teacher exits the auditorium, Ashley comes alive. He shouts, "Yeah, well blow me, then."

"There's still a lady here," Zo says just before he throws Ashley to the ground.

Ashley swings and connects on Zo, and the two tumble around onstage trying to kill each other.

"Needs work," says Miss Amenny.

I say, "Yeah, but the ending has promise."

I figure my next trip down to the junior high is gonna be for the sole purpose of collecting props and costumes. When I arrive in the At Risk room, I find Zo and Thad sword-fighting lackadaisically as usual. Everyone else is sitting around the edge of the room with these momma-just-croaked looks on their faces.

"Okay, everything in the box," I say as I unfold

the cardboard television container I brought with me. "Please fold up your costumes first, unstring your bows, and put the swords in their holsters."

"Sheaths," corrects Lissy.

"Yeah, what she said."

The swordfight stops, and Zo gives me this look like I'm crazy. Other students are already putting their stuff in the box.

"Why?" he demands.

"What do you mean why?" I say semibaffled. "Remember yesterday? No one wants to be in this play. *You* just want to get out of highway cleanup. Not me. I'd rather clean bedpans than watch you embarrass yourselves."

"So you're just gonna quit?" Zo says.

"Hey, I'm the last one in the room to quit. Except Phuong maybe. Everyone else threw in the towel yesterday. *You* were the first one to quit. You're the one who dragged his horse behind him. After that, you think anyone else in here was gonna try?"

"That horse is stupid."

"That horse was the best actor in the play."

"Man . . . " Zo says, shaking his head.

"What?"

"You don't understand?"

"Make me."

"Yesterday was easy. They could laugh all they wanted. You know why? Because they could tell we didn't care."

I think back on junior high for a second. I

remember actually giving a shit whether I wore Wranglers, or Levi's, or the Kmart brand we could actually afford.

"You know what?" I say as much to the whole cast as to Zo. "Back when I was going to school here, if I got handed a test, I might know half the answers. Sometimes more than that. But you know what I'd do? I'd just leave the whole thing blank or fill in the names of the Seven Dwarves instead of the Supreme Court, or whatever, because I figured it was better to look like I couldn't care less than look to stupid. But it didn't matter. They still thought I was stupid."

I can tell by some of their looks that they'd done the same thing.

"Look," I say. "I'm not gonna have us go look foolish for four straight weekends just for my ComServ credit. There are easier ways to get it than this."

"Give us another shot," Lissy says.

"Yeah," says Zo.

I look around the room at the rest of the cast. They all look like they're waiting for an answer from me.

"Are y'all gonna do what I say?"

There's a bunch of nodding.

"Even if it doesn't make sense to you?"

More nodding. I press my luck.

"I'll do it if Ashley wears tights."

"In hell," says Ashley.

"He'll do it," says Zo.

"Okay," I say. "But the first time anyone doesn't do what I tell him, I'm walking."

They get serious looks on their faces like they're trying hard not to laugh.

"Get up onstage," I order.

They do, but as he's walking past me, Zo whispers, "Just don't make us do it in front of those jackrabbits again."

When I blow the whistle everyone looks at me. That's the rule, and for the most part, they're following it. I'm blowing the whistle I borrowed from Miss A a lot. I figure the first problem I need to deal with is how this supposed "action" play is dragging, so the first thing I do is make the cast kick the show into what Miss A calls "lightning-time." Every line, every entrance and exit, every facial expression, every swing of a sword has to be delivered as fast as they can possibly do it.

I carry a stopwatch and give daily timings on the complete run-through. By the end of the first week of speed training, the same Robin Hood it took them forty minutes to do in front of an audience is over in eight. The show's not really any good yet, but they're enjoying it more when they do it fast.

Mrs. Doyle watches a little bit of the rehearsal during one of our speed sessions. She whispers to me. "I don't blame you, Tommy. I'd want to get out of there as soon as possible myself."

After the first week, we also practice with a standing no-stop rule, which means they're not allowed to call for lines or break character to ask me questions.

It also means they have to cover for each other if someone misses a line. The better they get, the more new rules I put in. If I blow the whistle and yell "lightning," they go back into the fast mode. If I say "molasses," every movement is performed in super slow motion. I throw them a curve one day and yell "backward." Travis looks down from the stage at me like I'm crazy, but Dodie catches on right away and repeats the line he's just finished saying, then he pours "ale" back from his glass into a pitcher. Travis clues in and says the line that came before Dodie's. They're actually able to make it back about three lines before they get hopelessly lost. Still, it's better than I hoped for.

At this point, I still haven't fixed our number one problem. They're not really acting. They're still just spinnin' out lines in their own boring voices without any real spark.

So, I pull another trick out of Miss A's book.

I tell them I want them to quit tryin' to act out Robin Hood, that from then on, when I give them a word, they'll have to do the play in that style. After that, if I yell "Western," the characters spit a lot, drawl their lines, and swagger around like a bunch of John Waynes. If I whistle, then yell "monster movie," I end up with a Friar Tuck with a pretty decent Transylvanian accent, a Robin Hood who howls after his lines, and a dead-on Witch Marian. The most helpful exercise, though, comes when I yell "soap opera." Following this guideline, they overact hilariously, and it seems to finally get them to loosen up. It's a week before I actually blow my whistle and yell "Robin Hood."

Miraculously, they just dive right in. Suddenly they're acting. There's anxiousness and volume in Daryl's voice when he delivers his one line, "Robin! Look out!" Lissy actually sounds less like a debutante and more like an English maiden. But the best part turns out to be Zo. Suddenly he's commanding the stage like he does the classroom, just oozing the confidence and swagger of a natural hero.

While I'm payin' attention to the acting, the cast members who aren't onstage spend their downtime rechoreographing the fight scenes. Every time I see Will and Robin's swordfight or Little John and Robin's quarterstaff battle, a couple new moves have been plugged in—leaping, somersaults, sliding. The actual weapons have become a blur. It's Dodie's idea to cut the tips off of arrows, fill up tiny balloons with ketchup packets they've snarked from the cafeteria, then have all the victims of death by arrow (Daryl and Phuong have five death scenes between them) swing the staffs up to their chests and puncture the balloons. Carnage happens. The fights, I have no doubt, are the best scenes in a show that's starting to look pretty damn good.

If I say so myself.

Miss A lets me drive the big school district van to Magnolia, home of the festival. She's supposed to be behind the wheel, but her eyes, she says, aren't what they used to be. I half expect the cast to be climbing all over each other in the backseats. Instead, they're just sitting there like wooden Indians. I want to believe they're concentrating, getting themselves psyched for their first real shows, but I know better — they're scared.

A festival representative wearing a Viking costume meets us at the gate and leads us across the thirty-acre Renaissance grounds. I'm as wide-eyed as my cast. I was sort of expecting a few tents and a couple hundred drunken slobs like we get during Deerfield's annual three-day chili cook-off, but it's more like walking through a medieval Disneyland. There are hundreds of booths selling everything from real armor to belly dancing outfits. Everyone who's working at the festival is dressed up. The pretzel girls are peasants. Ladies with mucho cleavage serve honey wine in taverns called The Welcome Wench or The One-Eyed Dragon. Teenagers do their best at yelling, "Get your tuhkey legs, suh" sounding like Beaumont-raised Oliver Twists. The scariest part of all: There're thousands of people here, and every third or fourth person is in costume. I count six or seven Robin Hoods by the time we get to our stage.

The Viking shows us the schedule that's posted on the backside of the children's stage walls. We're doing three shows a day for the next four Saturdays. "Should get full houses, it's such a beautiful day, thank Valhalla," he says as he scans the sky for rain clouds.

"You have forty minutes until your first show."

I look back down in time to see Dodie throwing up. "Nerves," I tell Thor.

But Dodie survives the first production of *Robin Hood*, and so does the rest of the cast. It's a bit tentative, but the first sword-fight gets a smattering of applause. Then the audience, mainly little kids with parents, laugh when Friar Tuck jiggles a stolen coin pouch and tells the rest of the Merry Men that they should also "shake their booty." By the time the finale rolls around, and a dying Robin instructs Little John, "Wherever this arrow may land, open Robin the Hood's Fish-n-Chip Stand," it's tough to tell who's enjoying themselves more, the audience or the cast. Little John, cradling the lifeless body of Robin, watches the imaginary arrow fly, grimaces, then wipes a tear from his eye and delivers the final line of the show. "Should I move the dead child first?"

The crowd whistles and claps. It's at that point that I realize I haven't had the cast rehearse a bow. Dodie and Zo get up from the stage, glance at each other self-consciously, and then walk back through a hole in the forest backdrop. No one reappears on stage, and the crowd, scratchin' their heads, slowly escapes without having to cough up any dollar bills into hats.

Miss A walks behind the stage with me. I'm expecting to find them whoopin' it up. Instead, they're all just standing back there with these looks of wonder plastered across their faces. I try to guess how many of them have ever had someone clap for anything they've done before.

"Twenty-four minutes," I announce. "You rushed it a bit. I'd like to see it come in closer to thirty."

"What?!" says Travis.

"Why you wanna say something like that?" says Ashanti.

"Pendejo!" says Thad.

"Gotcha," I say. "Y'all killed 'em. Now come out here. There's one more thing y'all need to learn."

And I show them how to take a bow.

As we're heading back out to the van that night, we practically fall into someone else's show. Two guys dressed fruitier than even I would dare with plumed Shaft Goes to Coventry hats, butt-hugging lavender velour pants, and rouged, eyebrow-plucked mugs have set up shop right in the middle of a field. Zo nearly knocks over one of the huge beer mugs they've used to stake their territory.

"Watch thy step, piglet. A stein is a terrible thing to waste."

It's obvious Fruitio here is joking, but something about getting called piglet doesn't set too well with Zo. "We'll see if you're all that," he says.

So our whole group sits down on the grass. I look on the schedule to see what these guys are called, but the program only lists what's on the stages. When they start, there's hardly anyone gathered. *A lot fewer than we draw,* I'm thinkin'. But, for the next twenty minutes they rattle off punch lines like a pair of cross-dressed Buddy Hacketts. They recruit a fat guy, a bald guy, and a hot-looking drunk Aggie coed as additonal characters. All the while they keep up a sword duel that sounds like a bushman debating team in action. I'm laughing so hard, I can't catch my breath between jokes. So's the rest of the cast of *Robin Hood*.

"So why don't they give those guys a stage?" Zo asks on the ride home.

"Because they don't need one," I tell him.

We start raking in the cash once the cast members know they're supposed to pass a hat. An average show nets us about four hundred dollars in wadded-up bills and quarters. As I predicted to Miss A, the Davy Crockett Jr. High At Risk kids are expert pan-handlers. They'll tell whatever lie they need to in order to weasel an extra dollar or two from a specta-tor. Sometimes they're all orphans who hitchhike from festival to festival to feed themselves. Occasionally they tell people that Phuong needs surgery if he's ever going to speak again. My favorite has to be the one where they say they're the Crockett Quiz Bowl Team and they're trying to raise money to go to Nationals.

"What *is* the money for?" I ask Miss A when I hand her the latest take.

"General drama fund," she tells me.

"Boring," I say.

By the time the third weekend rolls around, we've developed a bit of cult following at the festival. It's not just the kiddies draggin' their parents to the show. We're startin' to get regulars. Word of mouth is out about the Robin Hood show. Lately kids start lining up about twenty yards to the right of the stage, and when Robin fires his final arrow, they stage their own elaborate death scenes, clutching their hearts, making gurgling noises, and spinning completely around three or four times. The first time a kid did it, Zo, who was, by all rights, dead, couldn't keep from laughing.

The show and cast, by the time of the fourteenth or fifteenth production, has gone through a number of changes. Some good. Some not so good.

During the second week, Daryl picks up what I'm told is a lute at a craftsman's booth. He strums it a few times, and I'll be damned if he can't play the strange-looking thing.

"If it got strings, I makes it sing," he says.

I know the line comes from a movie; I just can't remember which one.

The kid may not read Faulkner, but he can play anything he hears a couple times. The impressed craftsman says we can borrow the lute if we'll just mention his booth at the end of each of our shows. I write in a new part for a Merry Minstrel. Let me tell you, you haven't lived until you've heard a lute rendition of "Foxy Lady," which is what Daryl starts playing when Maid Marian makes her entrances. We even let Ashanti belt out a chorus of "The First Time Ever I Saw Your Face" when Little John heads off to battle. That brief moment in the sun gives her a whole new attitude about the show, and, I notice, a new opinion about which boy in the play is the most lovable.

"Daryl sure can play," she tells whoever will listen.

One of the things that strikes me funny is how now I can't get them to take their costumes off. Between shows, they run around the grounds still wearing the same ketchup-stained peasant shirts, feathered caps, and faded green tights they've just finished performing in. You should see how they soak it up when people tell them they liked the show or when they ask if they can take photos with the little hams.

It's that sort of attention, though, that's making my job harder. It's like I've created some sort of monster. They're so proud of themselves that it's starting to affect the show. They're starting to stomp all over each other's lines, or they'll overact to try to get the big laugh. I'm thinking I may have to shoot one of them just to scare the others.

Before the final show of the third week, Lissy says I'd better come back behind the stage. I find Travis splayed out on the ground asleep. I shake him a bit to wake him up. It's no use. I sniff the cap of Friar Tuck's wineskin. At least I have my answer. It ain't grape juice.

"No show," I announce, a little pleased maybe,

thinking that this might teach all of them a lesson.

The cast members left standing grumble and complain. Ashley starts kicking Travis's body. Not real gently either. I do a double take at Ashley. First of all, he's added a big plumed hat of his own to his outfit. Second, he's got a tattoo I've never seen before. I grab his arm, partially so Travis won't end up bleeding internally, and partially to get a closer look. Inked out across his tricep are two banners pierced by a sword. On the top banner it says, THE SHERIFF. On the bottom one, TAKES NO PRISONERS.

"Tell me that's fake," I say. "Your parents are gonna—"

An unfamiliar voice cuts into my sermon.

"I'll play Friar Tuck."

I turn back around and see it's still my cast standing there, but they're all staring at Phuong.

"Phuong, was that you?" I say.

"I know the lines," he says without a trace of accent. "And I'm hardly ever onstage at the same time as Travis."

The rest of us are standin' there harelipped.

"All right," I say. "Do it then."

And the play comes off just like usual. Miss A has forced Travis to drink a bunch of natural vegetable juice they're selling at one of the booths. He's sitting in the crowd between the two of us. Afterward, the cast is walking around like little king shits. All of them, except for maybe Daryl and Phuong, let Travis know how they didn't need him.

"I guess y'all won't mind if I set up another show

back at Crockett, then?" I ask. "We can show those jackrabbits some real theater."

And just as I suspect, they sort of crumble in front of me. They make a bunch of excuses why they don't want to and how they don't have to prove anything to anyone.

As they slink away, Miss A speaks up. "Be careful you don't break their spirit, Tommy."

"They're better when they're humble," I tell her.

"Lord, lord, lord," she says. "There's never a tape recorder around when you need one."

She laughs. Then for some reason, she hugs me.

In honor of our final show, I get all the cast members presents: little plastic bows and arrows that'll remind them of their countless hours, new friendships, and unforgettable memories—at least for the next couple weeks until they lose the arrows or break the bows. The gifts only cost like three bucks each. What the hell? One night shift at Whataburger and they're paid for. I also get a dozen roses for Miss A and have the cast sign a card. It seems like all of the kids write how they can't wait to take her class when they get to Lee. Miss A is beaming, but I don't think it's just the card. She's brought along some bearded man who seems just as interested in theater as she is.

The Crockett At Risk Players don't get me anything, but what was I expecting? It's not like they know any better.

As the play ends and the cast lines up to take their bow, I go down the line and try to guess how many of them might actually take Miss A's class. Which ones'll get stuck in vocational classes they're not interested in. Who'll get knifed. Which ones will flunk out because the money they make flipping burgers means more than the history quiz they probably won't pass anyway. Who'll get to walk the stage four years from now and get to toss up a square hat?

It's been three weeks since we wrapped, and I haven't felt much like going back to the junior high to pick up the costumes and props. It's like I want to remember all of the kids in the show standing up there taking bows, not sitting in some classroom sweating out chapter summaries. But Mrs. Doyle calls Miss A and tells her I have to get my butt over there after school. She needs that stuff out of her room.

Miss A lets me leave school early. There're only two weeks left, and we're not doing anything anyway. I make it over to the At Risk classroom, but no one's in there. I can't find the costumes or props either. I wander around the whole wing. I'm pretty pissed off when the bell rings dismissing school for the day. Now I'm gonna have to come back tomorrow. I make my way through the crowd of thirteen-year-olds, proud that I'm still taller than most of 'em. I take the main doors out of the building that leads to the faculty parking lot where I left my truck.

As I step out of the building, I hear the faint sound of an instrument I know too well. I look across the grounds and see the cast of *Robin Hood* in full costume stationed down by the bus circle. A crowd of students has already started to form a circle around them. I have to weave my way through a bunch of kids to get a good view. By the time I can see anything, Zo and Thad are in the middle of their swordfight, and the kids around me are goin', "Damn!" and "Did you see that?"

The cast is getting laughs where they're supposed to. I hear kids around me asking friends for rides so they don't have to catch the bus. One Goober standing near me, who's clutching this laptop computer backpack, starts jabbering about how Ashley Ford got busted in sixth grade for selling dope, but the kid he's trying to explain this to tells him to shut up. When Dodie says his last line, the crowd laughs some more. The laughter turns into applause as my expert bowers have their moment one last time.

As I walk back to the At Risk room with them, I swear some of their faces are gonna break if they keep smiling that way.

"Kicked ass. Took names," I tell them.

"Language, Tommy!" says Mrs. Doyle.

"Yeah buddy," says Zo.

"Maricon," says Thad.

The girls come back in from the bathroom after changing, and everyone starts bringing their costumes up to me. I'm also handed props, but everyone's chunking stuff at me at the same time, so it's hard to keep track. Somebody hands me one of the bows, but as I'm about to put it in the box I notice something funny. This isn't one of our cheap little props. This is a carved piece of ash nearly six feet long. I glance up and see that all my kids are staring at me. I look back at the bow and notice the engraving running lengthwise along its flat surface.

ROBIN HOOD—TOMMY PARKS, DIRECTOR

On both the top and bottom ends, etched into the wood, are turtles.

"We had a guy at one of the booths at the festival carve it," says Phuong. "It just got here yesterday."

Ashley reads my mind.

"All that money people was throwin' in our hats," he says. "Some of it was bound to fall out."

And that makes me laugh.

I climb the catwalk up to the little glass office, tryin' my best to ignore the smells and sounds of production. The two weeks since I graduated from high school have just ripped on by me like I was standin' still. Which I kinda was. I knock on the door to the office, then let myself in. The woman behind the desk is using colored pushpins to make a Texas flag on the bulletin board.

"The Chuckster in?" I ask.

"Chuck!" she yells.

The supervisor comes lumberin' out.

"Dan's boy!" he says.

"Tommy," I say.

"Ready for the big money, huh?"

"Not exactly," I say. "I decided to keep my job at Whataburger. I just came to get my transcript back."

"Whataburger needs to see a transcript?"

"Nah. I'm just stayin' on there for some spare cash. I'm goin' to college."

"How's that?" he asks.

"Scholarship."

The Chuckster laughs like I'm jokin'. I don't blame him. He's seen my grades. But he doesn't know about a friend of Miss A's who happens to be the director of theater up at Central. And he doesn't know about all the boring things Miss A does with the Lee High drama general fund.